Endless as the *Stars*

By

DOMINA ALEXANDRA

2021

Endless as the Stars © 2021 Domina Alexandra
Triplicity Publishing, LLC

ISBN-13: 978-1-970042-16-0
ISBN-10: 1-970042-16-8

Printed in the United States of America
First Edition – 2021
Cover Design: Triplicity Publishing, LLC
Interior Design: Triplicity Publishing, LLC
Editor: Miranda Campbell - Triplicity Publishing, LLC

Also by Domina Alexandra

I Belong With Her

A Night Claimed (Claimed Series book 1)

Omega Rising (Claimed Series book 2)

Love Undercover

I'd like to thank Triplicity publishing for giving me a platform to share my stories. My editor, Miranda Campbell; you rock. Thanks for all your suggestions and catching anything that would take away from Tia and Carina's story. And my three amazing friends, Marisol, Naomi, and Maria for helping me come up with options for a cover. Some suggestions will never be shared, but I know the ending was a success.

I dedicate this book to every paramedic/emt partner out there in the medical emergency world and my personal best, Steve. There's nothing more powerful than facing every call with someone you trust. And laughing through the ones you walk out baffled on. Anyone in the medical field knows what I'm talking about.

Prologue

"Get me out!" The aggression from the patient was heard loud and clear. He shook violently on the gurney, ankles and wrists placed in soft restraints. His face was flushed, eyes pinpointed from the drugs he'd been taking. "I swear…" he roared loud enough for Tia to wish for ear plugs. Tia tried never to place her patients in a box. It was a trap for treating her patients with addictions all the same or becoming indifferent to their situation.

The ambulance drew to a stop, Tia sneaking a peek out the back double sided small windows. They were at a stop light. "Hey, Paul. Remember, we're not the cops. We only have you in restraints for your protection as well as our own."

"That's bull shit," he sneered. He shook his arms, trying to break free. The gurney shook but never broke from its locked position.

"You good back there?" Bruce called out. He twisted, checking for her response.

Tia shifted forward so that he could see she was physically safe and gave a thumbs up just as their patient tried to grab her pants. "Whoa there, buddy." Tia sat back on her seat. The ambulance began to move again, and she counted the seconds in her head until they'd arrive. Preferably soon. Since picking up their patient from the gas station and having the fire department assist them in putting him in restraints, her patient had not calmed down.

"Can I check your vitals, Paul?" Tia held the blood pressure cuff up for him to see. She always asked for their permission.

His face skewed into a new platform of rage. "No!"

"We're five minutes out," Bruce shouted from up front.

"Thanks." Tia looked down at her patient. "You hear that. We're almost there."

"I don't want to go. Let me out!" Her patient continued to bellow. After the last word left his mouth his rage seemed to deplete, as if his mind suddenly switched gears. "Why do I have to go?" He asked in a pleading voice.

Tia moved from the side of him to the captain's chair directly behind him. She heard him begin to cry, groaning from his emotional agony. "Paul. You're not well. We only want to help. Let us." Tia picked up the intercom mic. "Hey Paul, I need to call the hospital, okay?" He continued to cry, and Tia took her chance to call the hospital before he went back to screaming. "This is Medic 111 to Unity Memorial." As she gave her report, Tia watched as his hands squirmed around, trying to search for a new way out. He was about to burst into a new fit of rage and she advised the hospital to have security present.

Finished, Tia slid around the gurney, sitting beside her patient again.

"You're taking me against my will," her patient argued.

After he tried to destroy the gas station and attack the employees, Tia knew he'd only have a few hours of freedom before the cops would come and arrest him in the hospital.

"Let me out, now!" he bellowed. He tried to reach for her leg and then spit at her. Tia slid fast across the bench barely escaping his unsuccessful attempt.

"Bruce," Tia called out.

"I read your mind partner. Give me one second." Bruce pulled over and helped her place a spit bag over their patient's head. No one wanted a spit bath.

As she waited for her partner to come to the back, a headache began to emerge at the back of her head from all the emotions her patient expressed. She looked at the time on her wrist watch and sighed. *Another 11 hours to go in the start of her 12 hour shift.*

*

"Bro…" Tia chuckled. "I seriously went to sleep with a dozen personalities in my head. I had a dream I was on a boat cruise with every one of our patients. Trapped." Tia and Bruce were sitting at the dining room table connected to one side of the living room.

Bruce took a bite of his burger just as Tia finished her story and began laughing in hysteria when she finished. She noticed his eyes widen as he coughed harshly. He was choking on his burger and stood, stomping his foot on the tiled floor as if that would help him cough it out.

"Tia, help him," Carina said, concerned as she saw her husband struggle to breathe.

Bruce coughed two more times and then gasped as his wife patted him harshly on the back. She smacked his back again, not sensing that he'd recovered. "Ouch, babe." He winced, arching out his chest and took a step from his wife. "Why are you beating on me?" He reached for his glass of soda, swallowing most of it down his aching throat. Bruce shook his head as if Carina beat him on the regular.

All while watching Bruce and his wife, Tia chuckled, sticking a fry in her mouth. "You weren't lying when you said Carina beats on you."

"Oh, you two." Carina picked up a fry from her husband's plate and tossed it at him.

"What'd I do?" He laughed, watching his wife closely for another slap, this time over his head.

Tia knew the number one thing to do when someone was choking and coughing at the same time, was to tell them to continue coughing. Bruce was a paramedic and she knew he could handle himself. He choked on his food once a week, so he was an expert. Going back to their conversation, Tia continued. "Seriously though, we had way too many emotional patients today. Total overload."

"Next shift, we'll request only patients who have diarrhea or feel like they have an allergy who aren't displaying any allergic reactions," Bruce teased her. Bruce was always great at reminding her of the perks in being in the healthcare industry.

In response, Tia flipped him off.

"Mom, Tia stuck her middle finger up at Dad," Rina tattled. She was Bruce's oldest daughter and *daddy's little girl*.

Bruce grinned, pleased by his daughter defending him.

"Tia, don't get in trouble in my house!" Carina yelled from the living room in a playful tone.

"Really?" Tia asked, pressing her hand to her heart.

Rina shrugged. "You take me to a Julia Michaels concert for my birthday this summer and I'll back you next time."

"Blackmail." Tia shook her head. "You see the kind of daughter you're raising?" Tia smiled and looked at her watch. It was almost eight and close to her bedtime. "I should get going."

"You are crazy," Bruce stated. He wiped his hands in a paper towel, standing back up. "We barely ended our shift a little over 12 hours ago and now you're going to work a double."

Tia shrugged. "I need the money," she argued.

"For what?" Bruce countered. He held his index finger up, going down a list and adding another in his rant. "You aren't dating anyone, so no girlfriend expenses. And you don't have some sick grandma to take care of. Are you finally listening to my wise advice and going to paramedic school next semester?"

Tia snorted. He'd been hounding her for over a year about going to paramedic school. They worked together as an EMT and paramedic crew and she was content. Being his partner for over three years, she had no desire changing to a new crew if she became a paramedic. Countless times, Tia relied on Bruce to have her back. And he knew she'd have his. They'd been on calls that ranged from cautious to very dangerous. It wasn't easy finding a good partner and Bruce was the best. Tia wasn't willing to give him up. She brushed her finger over her nose a few times and shrugged. "I just like working."

He planted his hands over his waist, searching her eyes for a better answer.

Carina walked over, saving Tia from Bruce's potential lecture. She wrapped her arms around his waist and he dropped his arms. "Leave her be. Tia will do what she wants when she wants. You hounding her won't change that." She smiled at Tia and winked.

Tia mouthed a *thank you* and stood, collecting her plate. She went into the kitchen and began cleaning her dirty dish. She stood alone and silent until Carina walked up. Tia looked up as Carina stood beside her and held out her hand. "Thanks for the save."

Carina opened the dishwasher and placed the plate inside. "Of course. He means well, as you know, but he just doesn't know when to quit."

Tia snorted. "Agreed." She dried her hands on the towel and turned to face the dining room. "I should get going."

"He is right about one thing," Carina said in a supportive tone. "You should take a breath. Go out and have a day to yourself. Or you'll miss out on something special."

"Something or someone?" Tia grinned, knowing what Carina was trying to say.

"Both," Carina said. Bruce entering her life was the best thing that could've happened to Tia. He was the brother she never thought she'd have. The friendship she had with Carina was real too, as well as with their kids. "You, Bruce, and those kids of yours give me more than I've ever needed, but I'll keep what you both said in mind."

The kids were chasing after Bruce and screaming through the house. Carina shook her head and leaned against the counter. "Take me with you," she joked.

Tia patted her shoulder. "You chose this life," she said and headed out.

*

After working a double shift, Tia went home and planted herself in bed. She kicked off her shoes, staring up at the ceiling. Carina's words really stuck with her all shift. What would it hurt to take off one day? She practically worked six days a week. She tapped her fingers vigorously against the bed, deciding her fate. Tilting her head outward, she looked to the window, the sun barely coming up. She'd have to work her normal shift with Bruce tonight. Could he survive one shift without her? She smiled. Tia dug through her front pocket, heaving out her phone as she texted one of her coworkers who worked part time. He'd needed more hours. She offered him her shift for tonight and within minutes he accepted.

It was too late to change her mind. Instead of texting Bruce that she wouldn't be there, Tia figured it would be more entertaining knowing he'd look around confused about her whereabouts. He was always toying with her; it was about time she did the same thing to him.

Tia reached for the remote and turned on the TV, finding her favorite classic cartoon *Scooby-Doo*. She liked listening to it in the background as she fell asleep. She'd barely watched several minutes of it before her eyes drifted shut.

*

She woke up to the sound of her phone ringing. Tia tossed it further away from her, wanting to stay asleep. The phone began to ring again and Tia groaned. She reached blindly for it, getting irritated and shifted onto her elbow, blinking lazily to find it. It continued to ring as Tia scooted across her bed, picking up her phone right at the edge. She looked at the caller I.D. just as the call ended. She had five texts and three missed calls. One from the guy who was covering her tonight, one from her supervisor, and the other from an unknown number.

Alarmed by these many calls, Tia twisted, kicking the blankets off her body just as her phone began to ring again. She didn't bother seeing who it was, answering quickly. She looked at the time on her watch as Bruce's wife cried out to her in panic.

"What's wrong?" Tia asked, the pit of her stomach swirling and twisting into knots. She could sense the fear in Carina's tone expecting an emergency to have occurred with one of Bruce's kids.

"Oh God, I thought you were with Bruce tonight," Carina cried.

It was after eight and Bruce started his shift two hours ago. "No. I took your advice and called out. What's wrong?"

Carina continued to sob, trying to speak. "He was…shot…" she cried out.

Tia nearly dropped the phone from her hand. Her throat clogged and the ability to breathe was removed from her memories. Long seconds passed before she gasped for a breath and tears fell from her eyes. "Where…where are you?"Tia stuttered. So many thoughts were attempting to force their way into Tia's mind but she pushed them out when she heard Carina speak again.

"My sister's watching the kids. I'm on my way to the hospital."

Once she learned which hospital, Tia said she'd be there and leapt out of bed, nearly forgetting to put on her shoes. She scurried out of her apartment, fearing the worst as she drove to the hospital.

Two of her supervisors, a few coworkers, and a fire crew were seated in the waiting room of the ER. Tia rushed up to Dean who'd covered her shift. His face was pale, eyes webbed with tears. "What the hell happened?" Tia looked to him for an answer, ready to shake him if he didn't speak right away. He sat in the chair, his face in shock. He was wearing ER scrubs. That was a clear sign he'd gotten a lot of blood on him and had to change. The thought of losing Bruce was unnerving as Tia pleaded with the universe for him to be okay. The one night she chose not to work and he was shot.

"Tia…" Carina sobbed.

Tia turned, Carina rushing through the ER entrance doors and into her arms. "Where's my husband?" She cried in her arms.

Tia searched for a nurse and found one she knew. They locked eyes, and the nurse mouthed, *I don't know*, understanding what Tia was going to ask. That meant the trauma doctors were still working on Bruce. Tia could feel Carina's entire body shaking from fear, doing her best to contain her own emotions. "He'll be okay. He has to be," Tia told Carina as she continued to comfort her best friend's wife.

Anger surfaced in her eyes, but Tia reeled it back in. The one night she chose not to work, and this happened. She should've been there to back him. Tia knew she needed to be here now for Carina and found them a place to sit and wait for a doctor to tell them if Bruce was alive or not.

Minutes turned into nearly an hour. They were seated side by side, Tia never letting go of Carina's hand. She wanted to find out what happened but chose to stay at Carina's side instead. Bruce wouldn't want her to leave his wife alone. Carina didn't need to hear the details right now. Tia tapped her feet vigorously on the hard surface floor. More of her coworkers appeared over the hour along with a few police officers and members from the fire department. Bruce was loved by so many and well respected.

The anxiety of not knowing bothered Tia the most. She began cracking her knuckles and Carina reached over, trying to calm her movements. Their eyes locked and Carina wiped away a tear that fell from Tia's eyes. Tia sighed, shaking her head. She was supposed to be the one supporting Carina not the other way around.

Several more minutes passed when the double doors that led to the ER opened. Carina and Tia leapt up at the same time. Everyone stayed back, not wanting to invade the space meant for Carina.

Carina's grip tightened and pulled Tia forward. The doctor walked up slowly, one of the nurses beside her, and fear slammed into Tia's heart. Her eyes watered, her body trembling with trepidation. The doctor recognized Tia, their eyes locking briefly before shifting to Carina.

There was no mistaking the grief in the doctor's eyes as she spoke softly. "Mrs. Simpson…"

The doctor said no more as Carina screamed, dropping to her knees. Tia collapsed with her, reaching to pull Carina into her arms. They cried together unable to hear the rest. The pain was unbearable as they both choked out sobs that couldn't be controlled. Tia squeezed Carina tight, not wanting to let her go.

Minutes passed when a nurse approached, kneeling beside them. She tapped Tia's shoulder. Tia looked up, Carina's face buried in her neck. "Would you both…?"

Tia knew what she was asking. Tia nodded, clearing her throat. Trying to blink away the tears was hard as they kept falling. "Give us a moment," she whispered weakly. She brushed her hand over Carina's back. Slowly, Tia sucked in a breath trying to sound strong for Carina's sake.

"You want to see him?" she mumbled to her best friend's wife.

After a few sniffles, Carina nodded. After a long minute they stood and began to slowly walk, not emotionally ready to see his lifeless body. As they neared the trauma room, Tia nodded, thankful to the nurses who cleaned up whatever mess they made trying to save him. His body was covered with a few thick white blankets, only his face exposed. He looked asleep. Tia almost called his name, hoping he'd wake up and answer.

Carina cried harder, unable to step into the room. She shook her head, turning and resting her back against the wall. "I...I can't." She sobbed, eyes red and puffy. Her nose was running.

Tia reached over, using the sleeve of her shirt to wipe Carina's face. She squeezed her fist, released, and took a breath. Tia cupped Carina's face, forcing her to make eye contact. "This is an important decision you have to make. Don't leave without saying goodbye." Tia let out a shuddering breath, begging herself not to cry again. Not now. Her best friend was gone but Carina had lost her husband. The father of her children. Tia needed to help Carina through this next step.

Carina's body shook as she choked out a sob, covering her face. "But I don't want to say bye."

There was no hiding from the truth. Tia needed to make sure Carina didn't do that. She'd need to tell her kids and couldn't do that without facing this truth. Tia removed Carina's hands from shielding her face. "You have to. You have three kids waiting for you."

Carina took a moment and nodded, looking back to the room where her husband lie unmoving. *Lifeless.* They walked in and when they reached his body Carina's hands shook, reaching to touch his face. "He's still warm," she cried out. She leaned in and kissed his forehead.

For some time, Tia watched, her eyes on her best friend, part of her pleading for a miracle. Gradually, she backed out of the room and pulled out Carina's phone. After receiving so many calls and texts Carina didn't want to be bothered anymore. She called one of Carina's sisters, telling her the outcome. Her sister was now on her way, the kids staying with her husband.

Minutes passed when Carina's sister walked up. "She needs you." She squeezed Tia's arm and walked into the room where Carina lingered next to her husband.

Tia watched as Carina twisted into her sister and fell into her arms. There was nothing more Tia could do for Carina and she found no purpose in being there. The longer she stayed the more guilt she felt. She should've been with him tonight. Tia looked back at Bruce's unmoving body and felt herself shattering. She'd no longer be able to hear his jokes or watch his silly expressions. Seeing him like this hurt. Part of Tia felt as if she was in a dream. She stumbled away from the room, heading to the nearest exit. A few of her coworkers called her but she ignored them and left without looking back.

Chapter One

Four Months Later

Carina

A loud bang came from downstairs. Carina ignored it, walking to the bathroom. Her brunette hair was in disarray and tangled. She was headed to the toilet but stopped by the shadow of her figure in the mirror. She knew her brunette hair was a mess, brown eyes hollow. Carina lost a little weight from not eating enough, wearing oversized clothes to hide her curves.

Without Bruce, Carina felt lost and absent from the world. He'd been her rock for almost 15 years. Now, at 35, she was alone with no sense of direction.

One of her kids knocked harshly against her bedroom door. Carina planted both hands over her sink, wanting to climb back into bed.

"Mom!" Rina screamed through her door. "Johnathan freaking kicked his soccer ball in the house and knocked the TV over."

Carina shut her eyes, not answering her daughter right away. With a long sigh Carina shouted from her bathroom with no intention of approaching her bedroom door. "Okay. Be out soon." She shut herself inside the bathroom, sliding down the door to the floor. Carina wore her husband's shirt, bringing the hem of it up to her nose. All she knew how to do was cry. Her family was broken. It had been four months, but it seemed like just yesterday she lost her husband. The one person she could count on.

After 10 minutes of crying, Carina got dressed without showering and went downstairs. She ignored the mess that was made. Her kids stared at her but said nothing.

"Get your things." She walked to the car, waiting for them to follow. They argued the entire ride, Carina zoning out from their back and forth bantering.

After dropping them off at school, Carina went back home and curled into bed. She couldn't sleep, lying in her husband's shirt for the next two hours. She eventually got up, heading downstairs to check her mail. There were a few envelopes in her mailbox. One by one she skimmed over them and tossed them onto the kitchen counter until finding one letter unaddressed. Opening it, she found a check inside for $800. Carina closed her eyes and placed the check on the counter.

She looked to the living room and began to clean up the mess her son made. Johnathan was nine and her only son. He looked just like his father. In the past few months, that sweet smile he usually carried turned into anger and bitterness. He had random outbursts that she knew she needed to deal with before it was too late.

Carina ate a small meal and headed back into the bedroom to sleep the rest of the day away. Before she knew it, the kids were back, asking about dinner. Tonight, Carina knew she would order more pizza with arguing followed behind. She couldn't handle it. Not tonight. Carina called her sister to come and pick up the kids. She needed a night alone.

Once her kids were gone, Carina sat at the dining room table holding the check in her hand. Her husband had put in for life insurance, but she was unable to touch it yet.

Even if she had access to it, she couldn't. Just another thing to remind her that he was gone. But this check hurt her just as much and it wasn't the first one. She needed the money but was too angry to cash it.

She climbed into her car and drove until she reached her destination. She found a few ambulances parked outside the medic station getting ready to leave soon. There were a few employees she recognized. They smiled weakly but said nothing. Carina left her house in sweat pants and Bruce's shirt. She felt like a mess but didn't care at the moment. Once she reached the medic unit Bruce worked for the last four years, she opened the back door to the ambulance.

Tia sat on the bench seat alone, checking over her equipment. Her dark brown eyes widened, surprised by her presence. "Carina—"

"How dare you?" Carina spat out the words, not caring who was listening. "You think this is what we need from you?" She waved the envelope in her hand.

Tia stepped out of the ambulance, tears threatening to spill. She couldn't speak.

"Take your money." Carina shoved it into Tia's chest. Tia had been sending her money every two weeks for the last two months. Carina never spent a dime of it, holding on to it until now. She was finally ready to be angry.

"That's for you and the kids. I can't—"

Carina screamed. "Damn it, Tia. Take your money." She was about to fall apart. After losing Bruce she'd also lost her friendship with Tia too. At least, that's how it felt.

"No!" Tia retorted. "It's for you."

"You think this is what we need from you?" Carina let the envelope fall on the ground and turned to walk away.

An audience was building as the supervisor and a few employees stepped out.

Carina walked faster to her car, shutting herself inside as if it would block the feelings spilling out of her. She knew she looked crazy. She began crying, slamming the palm of her hand repetitively against the steering wheel. There was a knock on her window. Carina didn't roll it down afraid she might crumble.

The door opened, Tia kneeling beside her. Tia lowered her head, guilt soaking into her eyes. "I'm sorry."

Prematurely and out of anger, Carina slapped Tia harshly. A sob escaped Carina as she covered her face. Tia reached inside, pulling her into a hug. Carina consented for a brief time, but then pulled away. "No!" she hissed out. "I don't need you comforting me only to abandon us tomorrow." Carina hadn't realized until now how hurt she was from Tia abandoning them after Bruce's funeral.

"I wasn't..." Tia stopped and took her time. "After the funeral...it was hard looking at you all. I failed—"

"Don't you dare!" Carina shook her head, baffled by Tia's omission. "We needed you Tia, and you disappeared on us for the last four months. My family is torn apart." Carina never blamed Tia for her husband dying. All she wanted was her friend and Tia had disappeared.

Tia nodded, staring at the ground. She wiped her face with the back of her hand. "What do you want me to do? I thought I'd hurt you all by staying around."

"We needed you more than your money." Carina's voice came out rough and fractured. Carina wiped away her tears and reached out to wipe away Tia's. She missed her. "We still need you. The kids. I don't know what to do."

Courage built in Tia's brown eyes as she faced Carina's. She took a long breath, trying to find a way to make up for her cowardice. "I'm sorry. I thought—I was wrong to leave you alone. Bruce…he'd hate me for it."

"We need you. And you need us," Carina spoke firmly. She looked one last time into Tia's eyes. "Dinner will be at six tomorrow night."

Tia stepped back and nodded.

She closed the door for her as Carina put on her seatbelt and drove off.

Chapter Two

Tia

"You need a minute?" Quintin asked. He was one of many temporary partners Tia had lately.

Working Medic Unit 111 was her normal shift of six pm to six am. Once she got back to work, there had been a string of paramedic's covering Bruce's shifts. And none Tia cared to work with. It wasn't easy finding a great partner. Tia had that with Bruce and now he was gone. She shifted the gear into drive and took off with Quintin, only looking forward.

Sometimes a call would pop up at the start of shift and other nights they could sit posted at a location for hours waiting for their first call. That was tonight. It'd been almost three hours and the night was still silent. She stuck her ear phones in her ears, ignoring any chance of making conversation. She didn't want to. Quintin was a funny guy, but nothing could make her laugh since Bruce died. She'd never had to work with Quintin before.

A call rang, their phone vibrating as dispatch sounded on the intercom. "This is dispatch to Medic Unit 111. You have a call coming from 225 Church St. An officer assist for a K-9 bite."

Quintin reached for the mic, but Tia moved faster, snatching it up. "This is Medic 111. We copy call. En route."

"When we get there, can you—"

"I know what to do," Tia cut off. "It's a freaking dog bite," she muttered.

She heard Quintin sigh, but he said nothing. It took them a few minutes to arrive. She parked the rig and walked around back to grab the medic bag.

The police unit SUV was parked on the side of the road, its lights still flashing. The police officers' K-9 barked in the backseat as they approached. They had a suspect handcuffed.

"Can we temporarily remove the cuffs—"

Both the police officers and Tia said no at the same time. Tia looked to Quintin as if he was a rookie and she was his superior. He was a paramedic and Tia was the EMT. He had higher ranking, but she'd worked more years than him with all the experience he had as an EMT and paramedic combined. She knew she was being harsh but didn't care. Their patient was in handcuffs for a reason.

She walked up to the patient. "I'm Tia. An EMT. I'm just going to check out your hand."

"My knee hurts too. They slammed me to the ground." The patient looked up to her with pleading eyes as if asking she request to take him to the hospital.

She opened the bag, grabbing a small 500 ml bottle of sodium saline. She used her gloved hand to touch his wrist. Blood dripped from the palm of his hand. Skin was torn open from a few puncture marks. The patient hissed. She poured the container of sodium saline over his entire hand and used a thick patch of gauze to clean it up. She examined further, checking for coloration and anymore tears around his hand. "Wiggle your fingers," she told the patient. He did and she continued to clean, asking the cop to use his flashlight to see better. It was dark out and the red and blue lights from the police vehicle didn't help.

Hand clean enough, Tia used rolling gauze to wrap around the patient's hand. "All done. Were you planning to take him to the emergency room yourselves for a full clearance?"

"Yeah. We got it from here. Thanks."

Tia nodded. "Then my job is done." She removed the used gloves, tossed them in the trash bin in their ambulance, and put the bag away. Tia took out the Tough book they did their charting on and typed up a quick report. When she was done, she hopped in the front driver seat and grabbed the mic, clearing them from the scene.

Tia drove off, counting the hours until she'd be done with her shift.

*

At home Tia couldn't sleep. After losing Bruce, it took sleeping pills to give her at least five hours. It wasn't easy going back to work. After his funeral, Tia asked for leave, using much of her paid overtime to escape. There was no vacationing in her absence. Every night she cried, hibernated in her room watching endless TV. She'd gone to the gym practically every day. Depression worked differently for many. For Tia, it came out through anger and exercise.

Work reminded her of Bruce, but she needed to go back. She knew Carina and the kids would need the money and couldn't picture letting his family struggle. Seeing Carina last night brought back all her tears. Tia hadn't cried in the last month.

After showering, Tia stared at herself through the foggy mirror from the steam. The sight of herself obscured, she shut her eyes, not ready to really face herself. She'd only breakdown. Carina gave her a dinner time, not leaving much room for her to say no. If she didn't show up tonight, it could be the end of whatever friendship they had left. If she bailed, Tia knew Carina wouldn't take her money even more so. Carina was strong like that.

She found a hair band on the counter, twisting her long brown dreads into a bun. An inch was shaved off at the back bottom half of her head. Tia opened the door, cool air coming into the bathroom and breezing through her skin. The fog from the mirror dwindled but Tia couldn't bring her eyes up to look at herself.

Dressed, Tia looked at the time and headed out with a few minutes to spare. The drive filled Tia's lungs with anxiety, but once parked out front of Bruce's house, it flooded her and her hands began to shake. Could she do this? Walk inside his house again? Face his family?

The porch light turned on and the front door opened. Carina stood at the entrance, wrapped in a sweater. Tia stared at her best friend's wife and then down at her hands, trying to shake them free of tremors. This had to be done on her own. "Get out of the car." She chastised herself a lot lately. The engine shut off when she turned the key. Her body moved before her mind was emotionally ready to leave.

When she stood and turned to face the house, Carina was a few steps away. She studied Tia, opening her mouth to speak when they both looked toward the house. A loud, bitter scream came from inside. Carina shut her eyes as if hearing one of her children in that much emotional pain cut through her skin and stabbed her heart.

She looked up to Tia's eyes weakly and didn't bother putting on a smile. "I should go inside." She turned to walk and stopped. Carina waved her hand to Tia's car.

"Look, maybe I'm asking too much of you. After hearing that…" She pointed her thumb over her shoulder toward her house. "Why would you even want to step into my house? Maybe I'm being selfish. At this point, even I'm questioning why you'd want to be here." Carina's voice broke at the end of her last word. There was regret in saying it. She shut her eyes and shook her head, a tear slipping through.

Tia looked toward the house and realized how wrong she was to stay away. Bruce wouldn't want his family this way. He'd expect Tia to do right by him and take care of Carina and the kids. Tia stepped forward, holding out what she brought. "I have ice cream for the kids and a bottle of wine for us to soak in our misery later," she offered.

Carina opened her eyes and studied the offerings. A few heartbeats passed when she grinned and began laughing, realizing what she'd done. Carina couldn't remember the last time she laughed. "I guess you came prepared." She nodded toward the house, and Tia followed inside.

*

The reunion with the kids had been tough, the light in their eyes gone since losing their father. Especially the youngest Michelle. She was only seven and was once the most talkative of them all. Her smile brightened the world. Now, she said nothing, her head always down.

Tia watched as Michelle nibbled on her dinner. When ice cream was offered, she shook her head, keeping her eyes hidden from everyone.

"You think ice cream is going to make up for you ditching us like you ditched our dad?" Rina sneered. She crossed her arms over her chest and huffed, leaning back against her seat.

Her words cut sharp to Tia's heart as she looked across the table. She was Bruce's eldest. Tia always knew Rina had a sharp tongue, but she never pictured it being used on her.

"Rina. You need to watch yourself—"

Tia held up her hand. "It's okay," she assured Carina. It was important Rina got her anger out. Tia could handle it. At least pretend to. "I did abandon you guys. And I make no stupid excuses for it."

"Then admit it: you abandoned our dad too," Rina retorted. Her eyes were near ready to burst with tears. "You were supposed to be at work. To be his partner. He said you always had his back and you didn't." Her voice cracked and she stopped talking, turning her body in the chair away from Tia.

Johnathan's eyes hardened. "I don't want to talk about this!" he screamed out swiftly. His nose flared up as he breathed heavily, his chest caving in and out.

Tia brushed her fingers over her chin and gradually covered her mouth. She wanted to hide the stiff movement she made that would give away too much of her emotions. Michelle began to cry.

"I wish—every day—I was there." Tia wanted to be clear on her thoughts and intentions. She'd failed them the last four months. Carina didn't interrupt, and Tia took that as a sign that she could speak freely. "Your father—I loved him. The only brother I'll ever have." Growing up as an only child, Tia felt like she hit the jackpot meeting Bruce and his family. He opened her world to possibilities and new emotional connections. "I wasn't there and that will be something I have to live with. But I know he wouldn't want me blaming myself. He wouldn't want any of us blaming each other. None of us did anything wrong." That's what Tia kept trying to tell herself, wondering when she'd one day start to believe it.

"You disappeared," Johnathan said, arms crossed over his small chest. "That wasn't cool."

"No, it wasn't. And I'm sorry." Tia looked to each of the kids and over at Carina, expressing regret. Her look was somber and vulnerable. "I'm going to be here now. And no matter how angry you are at me...I'm not going anywhere, again."

Time slipped away and the kids finished their dinner, Tia carrying Michelle's sleepy body to bed. She tucked her in, giving her a kiss over her forehead. Michelle said nothing, turning her back to Tia and bundling into her blanket.

Tia sighed and promised herself never to leave them again. For a moment she lingered next to Michelle, running her fingers lightly through her hair.

Once the kids were in bed, Carina and Tia talked for a bit without saying much of anything. Tia eventually stood to leave and promised she'd be back. It was hard being here but Tia needed it. Once Carina was satisfied, Tia left hoping next time would be easier.

Chapter Three

Tia

It'd been a few weeks since Tia reintegrated back into their lives, picking the kids up from school any chance she got. The moment Tia stopped the car, the kids hopped out, Johnathan leaving the backseat door open. Tia climbed out of the car, calling his name. He turned, noticing the open door and ran back, shutting it.

"Sorry, Tia." He let his backpack dangle over his shoulder as he ran back to his house.

She chuckled, knowing he'd toss his backpack on the floor the moment he stepped inside. He'd been squirming for the last several minutes to go to the bathroom. She watched him fly past his mom as she stepped outside her home. Rina and Michelle walked past Carina, both with their heads down.

Tia let her arm hang over the car door, watching Carina approach. "So you know, I did give Johnathan a pre talking to. I figured you wouldn't mind me giving him my thoughts." Johnathan got in trouble at school for arguing with a classmate and then turning his anger onto his teacher.

"Of course. I appreciate it. It's good having someone else confirm to him what he did was wrong." Carina smiled and stared off to nowhere in particular.

Tia watched a tear slip from Carina's eyes and her smile faltered. A day could never go by without them thinking of Bruce. He was such a huge part of all their lives.

Carina sniffed, wiping her face. "Sorry."

"You don't have to—"

Carina waved her hand. "I know." She put on a brave face. "The last few weeks have been easier since you've come back. Thanks again."

Tia nodded and got back into her car incapable of saying more. Tia was thankful that Carina was giving her a second chance to make up for lost time. There was still a long road ahead for them, but Tia was glad she could learn to get through the days with Bruce's family at her side.

*

"You good with stopping at Starbucks?" Chuck was her third partner of the week.

One thing Bruce and her did right at the start of shift was go to Starbucks, betting on the way there if they'd get a call before their coffee. It was a gamble they both enjoyed making together. Tia hadn't been able to drink coffee at work since.

"No!" she said sharply. She knew she was being abrasive but that didn't stop her. She didn't want to create habits with new or temporary partners. Habits formed unexpected connections, and Tia had no desire to get attached again. Losing Bruce was more than she could ever handle.

"Look, Tia. I get that you're not happy about what happened to your—"

"Get the fuck out of my rig," Tia shouted, pressing her chest against the steering wheel and pointing toward his passenger side door. They hadn't left the station. Tia's fingers tightened around the steering wheel, tempted to punch him in the face. Just the mere mention of Bruce set her off if he was brought up in the context of her moving on.

"My bad. I didn't mean to go there. It's just—"

She was about to tell him to leave again when a call popped up. A 42 year-old female complaining of chest pain. In response, Tia picked up the mic, driving in route. Despite how she felt about Chuck, her potential patient took precedence.

It took her five minutes to arrive, the fire engine pulling up at the same time. Tia put on gloves, heading to the back of the rig to load the gurney with the airbag and cardiac monitor. Her partner grabbed the rest of the equipment as they headed inside the house. Their patient was lying in bed, her husband standing off to the side.

"How long have you been feeling this way?" One of the fire paramedic's asked.

The woman groaned, her skin flushed. "I noticed my heart racing. And then I couldn't take a normal breath."

Tia walked to the side of the bed, turning on the monitor and attaching her to the 12 lead ECG. She pressed a button for rhythm and handed one of the paramedics a blood pressure cuff. Her saturation read 90 percent room air. Tia scooted the cardiac monitor to the center of the bed, placing one knee on the bed to get closer to the patient. "I'm going to put you on about four liters of oxygen." Tia worked to put the cannula around her nose and ears.

"I'm going to start an I.V., okay?" Chuck alerted the patient.

"Have you taken anything for the chest pain?" Tia asked.

"I—" The woman thought about the question, her husband answering *no* for her.

Chuck spoke before Tia had the chance to ask another question. "Your heart's beating pretty fast. Have you experienced this before?" His question drew the woman to look down at what he was doing.

Their patient winced when Chuck poked her with the needle.

"Try to keep this arm still for me," Chuck told her, focused on pulling her skin back from her inner arm to get a better look at her vein.

"I'm going to give you some aspirin. Let's see how you feel after, okay?" Tia gave it to her, hoping it would help.

Two of the fire crew got the gurney prepped for transporting the patient over.

The patient's heart rate seemed to linger close to 200 beats per minute. There was no slowing down her heart rate without aggressive medication. It was concerning, and they needed to slow the rhythm.

"It's worrisome how fast your heart's going," the fire paramedic said. He shifted, allowing for both the patient and her husband to hear him clearly. "We need to give you something to slow your heart."

Chuck called out what he'd give her to slow her heart. "This medication is called amiodarone. You'll feel a little funny, but it'll slow your heart."

"I'm going to put on these electrode pads. We'll need to do what is called a cardioversion." Tia explained what that meant. "This combined with the medication increases the chance of the cardioversion's success."

Tia loved her job, and being here right now to help this woman was one of the few things she could do to escape her thoughts. Several minutes rolled by before their patient was on the gurney and in the back of the rig with a successful cardioversion. That ended on a good note.

*

Tia held out a check, waiting for Carina to take it. "Please don't say no. I combined all the other money you never cashed out into this check. Take it." Her brow furrowed, needing Carina to accept it. It was one of the few most important things that made her feel useful.

"What about you?" Carina asked, pointing to the check. "You certainly didn't make as much as Bruce." Her tone drifted to grief, but Carina wouldn't cry today. Crying turned into depression and her kids needed her to wake up. To be strong. "This is too much."

"I gave up my apartment and am staying with my dad. At least until I find a roommate."

Carina shook her head. "See, no, Tia!" She turned from the money offered, opening the fridge.

From what Tia could see, there weren't many options when she investigated the fridge. She wanted to argue until Carina took the money but quit for now. "Go!" Tia shut the fridge door on Carina and pointed at her watch. "You can't be late for your interview."

"When they wake up, tell the kids to clean their rooms. And to—"

"I've got this." Tia pointed to the door until Carina left.

It was Saturday morning and the kids would be up at any moment. Staring at the fridge, Tia contemplated how she'd utilize her time. Carina had two interviews back to back. Rubbing her palms together, Tia came up with an idea. She ran upstairs, skipping a few steps. She knocked and then opened Rina's door first, finding her asleep on the bed. "Rina!" she shouted. Rina's head stuck out from underneath the covers, twisting her head to face Tia standing at the door way. "Get up and help me get your brother and sister dressed. We're going out."

*

"Mom isn't going to like this," Rina pointed out for the third time.

They'd just arrived back to the house, Carina texting that she'd be home in an hour. There were still a few things left to do and Tia wasn't going to back out of her plans now. "You're saying she won't like that you all cleaned up the house and had lunch ready for her when she gets home?" Tia knew what Rina was referring to and would deal with Carina's disapproval when the time came.

"Go clean your rooms." Tia began putting the food away. She tossed a bottle of water to Johnathan and he caught it. "That's for you when you eventually try to make an excuse to come down those stairs. Clean your room."

Johnathan frowned, an attitude ready to make its appearance. He'd already had a tantrum when they went shopping. His temper was noticeable every time she saw him. "I don't see why it's a big deal to clean my room."

"Just do it, stupid!" Rina shouted.

"Hey!" Tia walked up to Johnathan who was about to rush up the stairs where Rina stood. She blocked him from going up. "First, we don't call anyone stupid!" Tia scolded. She stared up at Rina who sought no interest in apologizing and walked to her room. Tia shook her head and looked to Johnathan next. "If you really need me to answer your question, I will. Otherwise, you can go to your room and clean it."

Johnathan grumbled under his breath and stomped his way past Tia and up the stairs. She'd heard what he said, reminding her Bruce was no longer here. Tia let him head up without saying anymore about his attitude. She said what was needed and would wait till the right time when he was calm enough to listen. He wanted his dad and so did she.

Tia lingered by the stairs, her hand resting over her hip as she reminded herself Bruce was gone. A tear managed to slip past her barrier. When she turned to head back into the kitchen, she found Michelle standing close, noticing her sadness. She'd been caught crying in front of Michelle and it'd be a mistake to pretend she wasn't sad. Michelle needed to know it was safe and acceptable to cry and express how she felt. Tia knelt and smiled weakly at this young look-a-like of the best friend and partner she'd lost.

Her heart nearly stopped when Michelle reached across, using her small fingers to wipe away her tears. Tia opened her mouth to speak but knew this moment needed no words. To her, this was an improvement for Michelle. After she made sure Tia's eyes were dry, Michelle looked down at the stuffed bunny she held and handed it to Tia to keep.

There was nothing more tender than Michelle offering up such a gift. Tia held back her tears long enough for Michelle to walk up the stairs and to her room. Once she was alone, the emotions she'd been containing spilled out like a soda bottle exploding after being dropped. She sat at the dining room table, pressing her elbows atop the table and covering her face with her hand. Tia wondered if it would ever get easier. The front door opened and Tia looked up expecting Bruce to walk through.

Carina stepped into view, tossing her purse on the couch. Carina looked exhausted, kicking her shoes against the wall and taking a seat across from her at the dining room table. "What a—"

Twice Tia had been caught crying. She dropped her head, wiping her face. She'd been paralyzed with the hope of seeing Bruce; it was a reality kick when he didn't appear. There was silence between them as Tia inhaled. "Sorry. I was in my head." She stood, feeling awkward about being caught. It wasn't Carina's job to comfort her or to see her like this.

"You don't have to be sorry." Carina's voice was tender and understanding. She shook her head. "I still have all of his stuff in my room. I can't let anything of his go."

Tia nodded. "I should—"

"You don't have to leave."

"You're home early." Tia walked over to the kitchen, pulling a few ingredients from the fridge.

Carina followed, leaning into the island counter top in the center of her kitchen. "Yeah, the second interview was shorter than I expected." She watched Tia place cheese and butter on the counter. The expression on her face grew inquisitive. "So, uh…I don't think that second interview went well. They began asking me about my personal life and how available I'd be and I kind of broke down and walked out."

"Oh." Tia stopped what she was doing and studied Carina, checking for any signs she'd breakdown. Tia needed to be there for Carina and if she could help, she would. "How are you now?"

"How are *you*? I caught you in a pretty emotional state." Carina turned the conversation back on Tia and waited for an answer.

Tia smiled. "I asked you first."

"It's not every day anyone gets to see Tia Benson cry. But you've seen me cry on multiple occasions." Carina was being sincere.

"Yeah, well don't get use to it," Tia joked, wanting to loosen the tension. She'd never been someone who openly expressed her emotions.

"Why?" Carina wouldn't let this conversation slip away so easily.

Tia had no comeback. Her reasons for not wanting to cry in front of Carina or anyone would seem foolish. Tia knew Carina wanted her to be open.

"I told you. We need you…and you need us," Carina said softly.

Tia sighed and turned to grab a skillet as she heard the kids coming downstairs.

"Tia, my room's—" Rina stopped and shifted a glance to her mom. "I guess making mom a surprise lunch is ruined," she chimed out.

Carina grinned. "I was supposed to get a surprise lunch?"

"Well you kind of ruined that plan," Tia joked. "But how does grilled cheese and chips sound?"

"I don't think we have chips," Carina walked to the cabinet to check. She opened it and froze. "Seems we do." She turned and narrowed her eyes at Tia, all while pointing to her daughter. "Go upstairs."

Rina shook her head. "I told you she wouldn't like it."

Alone, Tia looked Carina in the eyes, not intimidated by her stare down. Bruce had warned her on many occasions how his wife could make him submit with her crazy stare downs. Tia could believe it, but she wouldn't falter. When Tia felt she'd done something right, no one could make her feel guilty for it.

"I told you, I didn't want to take your money."

"And you didn't take it." Tia placed the loaf of bread on the counter, but stopped to say what she was thinking. It was important she got her words out. "I get it. You don't want my help. No one's help. Financially, at least. I always knew that about you." Bruce had told her of their financial struggles. Tia had offered to help, but he'd declined. She knew right away it wasn't because Bruce wouldn't accept it. It was Carina who wouldn't. "I'm not asking you to pay me back. I don't want you to."

Carina shook her head, eyes tearing up. She looked away feeling vulnerable. "I just...I get anxiety about money. I know what happens when I go without it, but I also know what happens when I owe someone. That only creates more anxiety for me."

"I get it. My dad and I only had each other growing up. And when he'd get locked up for stealing food for us, I'd have to eat anywhere I could get food for free. It's a scary thing not having it. And scarier when you get it with strings attached." Tia walked up to Carina, wanting nothing more than to be honest. "I'm telling you. There are no strings. You and those kids are all I have. And of course, my dad too." She smiled. "I bought enough groceries to last the next month or two. I'm not great at calculating food and hungry kids."

Carina chuckled. "Bruce mentioned that."

They both laughed. Tia pointed upstairs. "I might've also bought things needed for the house and a few things for the kids."

"Tia." Carina shook her head. "That's too much."

"No, it's not!" Tia was adamant. "I love you guys and I need to know you're okay. Bruce would beat my ass if I didn't."

A small smile formed and Carina sighed. "Okay. I feel like I have to do something though to make—"

"You just...focus on you and those kids." Tia opened her arms and Carina went in for a hug. They both sighed, Tia realizing that she'd accepted her offer. There was mutual respect and Tia was thankful Carina allowed her to be here for them.

Chapter Four

Tia

Tia sat on the couch, eating a bowl of grapes. Her father walked over, slapping her foot off his coffee table. "Sorry," she said, not interested in what was on TV. Tia had a lot on her mind that she knew her father could see.

"Scoot." He waved his hand and she slid over as he took a seat. He was thin with salt and pepper short hair. Her father was in his late 40s but looked older than he was. A hard life could do that to anyone. "It's your one night off. You should be out socializing."

It had been a week since Tia last saw Carina and the kids. She'd had to work every day which was her own doing. There was no room to take breaks. "I'm good, Dad."

"You've sacrificed so much for…" Tia gave her dad an annoyed look and he frowned. "Don't give me attitude." He scooted to the edge of the couch, twisting to face her properly. "Not too many people would do what you're doing. I'm proud that you care so much and want to be there for his family."

"Then what are you saying?" Tia asked defensively.

"There's a way to do that without compromising too much of you. You still must live honey. Continue to connect with all your other friends. Make new ones. Fall in love."

Tia let out an audible groan, leaning further into the couch. "I knew that was coming."

"Did you now?" He grinned. "I need grandchildren."

Tia narrowed her eyes. "I don't think I need a partner to do that."

"I know. But you won't have a kid without one," he said knowingly.

Tia furrowed her brow. "I never said that."

"You didn't have to. It was hard on you, not having a second parent to lean on. When I messed up or fell apart, you had no second options. I could tell that hurt you. I'd hurt you. You want to make sure that when you have a child they have another parent to lean on." Her dad smiled and leaned in to kiss her cheek. "I also know that's why you're stepping up for Bruce and his family. Carina and her kids need you. But you still must live for you too."

Tia took in her father's words and quietly sighed. There was no denying it was hard on Tia growing up with only one parent in the house. She didn't like to think about the past and her mother walking out on them. Staying focused on the issue in front of her she finally acknowledged his words aloud. "I will," Tia promised. For now, she couldn't imagine going out and living her life when Carina and the kids weren't doing the same. That thought gave her an idea. "Thanks Dad. You'll be the first to know when I find that special one."

He grinned and got up. "I'm off to play dominos. Don't wait up."

Tia rolled her eyes. "Sure thing."

*

For the next hour, Tia flipped through the television channels considering her options for the rest of the night. It was still early and she had much time to do something. The thought of Bruce's family stuck at home, not having a good time dampened her mood.

Her phone rang, and Tia reached for it on the coffee table. When she answered, there was a length of silence before Rina's voice came on the line.

"Johnathan slammed his baseball bat into the wall and put a hole in it. Michelle is crying, and…shut up, Johnathan. Yes, I'm snitching."

Tia pulled the phone from her ear, hearing too much screaming on the other end. In search of her shoes, Tia rushed to the front door, knowing she didn't need to wait for an invitation to go see the kids and Carina. Something was clearly wrong for Rina to be calling her. "Where's your mom?" Tia asked, searching for her keys and wallet.

Rina wasn't paying attention, still arguing with her brother.

"Hey, Rina! Where's your mom?" Tia spoke authoritatively.

"She locked herself in her room, telling us to go to bed." Rina hissed. "But Johnathan got mad after and I don't know what to do."

"I'm on my way."

They exchanged a few more words, hung up, and Tia got in her car. It took her less than 10 minutes, driving above the speed limit, to reach the house.

Tia opened the front door, finding Rina on the couch with her little sister, her head lying over her lap. Tia whispered, not wanting to disturb Michelle's sleep. "Stay down here."

Upstairs, she heard pacing coming from one of the rooms. Tia turned to face Johnathan standing with the baseball bat in his hand. Carefully, she approached, holding her hand out. She peeked into his room, finding a few things destroyed. His lamp lay broken on the floor. His clothes were all over and he'd made a hole in the wall. His room looked like it was owned by a junkie. At nine years old, he shouldn't be filled with so much rage. But she could understand. Tia had wanted to put holes into walls too. At nine, expecting him to not feel anger for losing his father was foolish.

There was anger and fear in his eyes. "Give me the bat," Tia said softly. She wanted to make him feel safe, so she knelt to be at his level and extended her arm. Tia trusted he wouldn't attack her with the bat, but if he tried, she'd be fast enough to grab it. "Come on, buddy." Tia smiled, showing no anger in what he'd done.

Johnathan looked down at the bat he was holding, and it was evident he was tired. Tia was sure he was tired physically and emotionally of so many things. He took a step, lowering the bat and looked into Tia's eyes. "I didn't want to. But I got so angry."

"I know, buddy. I've been getting angry too." She had. At every paramedic she worked with. Tia gave them no chance to even want to consider being her permanent partner. That's what she didn't want. To have someone new and permanent take Bruce's position. "It's hard trying to smile when you want to scream."

He walked the rest of the way and took a breath. His eyes watered as he handed her the bat. Tia took it, immediately placed it behind her, and opened her arms. He studied her for a time and let tears fall as he planted himself into her arms. He cried, burying his face into the crook of her neck. Tia stood, carrying him downstairs. She went to the living room where Rina sat with Michelle who was still asleep.

"I love you, buddy. You, Rina, and Michelle." She sat with him in her arms for several minutes until he wiped his eyes and closed them sleepily. She let him stretch on the couch next to Michelle's balled up body on the other end, his head over her lap. Tia brushed her fingers through his curly hair until he relaxed enough to stop trembling with deep emotions.

Tia whispered to Rina, getting her attention. "Thank you for calling me."

"I knew you'd come." Rina sighed.

It warmed Tia's heart to know that in their time of need, Rina could lean on her too. The night was not over. Tia pointed upstairs. "I'm going to go up and talk to your mom."

Rina nodded.

On the way up, Tia thought of everything to say and came up with nothing. In the last three years of knowing Carina they'd never been close on an in-depth personal level until now. She knocked gingerly on the door. There was no answer. She pressed her ear against the door and knocked again. The door opened and Tia paused unsure if she should walk in. This was once Bruce and Carina's personal space.

Carina turned and sat on her bed. She used tissue to blow her nose. Her eyes were red and puffy. "This is embarrassing. You didn't have to come all this way."

Tia lingered in the doorway to Carina's and Bruce's room. It felt like an invasion if she crossed the threshold. The fear of crossing an emotional barrier paralyzed her to stay put.

"You can come in." Carina looked up.

"I don't think—I don't want to invade your space." Tia slid her hands in her front pocket.

"Tia. Please. I can't go out there just yet. I acted poorly as a mom."

In one step and after taking a breath, Tia entered the room. "You aren't a bad mom."

"I freaked out and shut myself from my own kids." She began crying, unable to maintain composure. "My kids are falling apart, and I failed them." Carina wasn't afraid to show her emotions as tears streamed down her face from all the hurt and fear she was enduring.

"You're not a bad mom." Tia sat beside Carina, offering a hand. When she took it, Tia squeezed firmly. "You lost your husband. They lost their father. Grief can make us do or say anything."

"Yeah, I just can't afford to screw up anymore."

Tia could understand that. "You're allowed to be angry. We all are." There was never a day Tia didn't want to scream. As an EMT she saw so much, but Bruce's death had taught her one thing. She exhaled, shuddering through the anger building in her gut. "You know what I hate the most?" she asked quietly.

It was in Carina's eyes, the concern of seeing Tia so frustrated by her own thoughts. "What?"

Elbow pressed into her thigh, Tia cracked her knuckles from all the anxiety that started to cloud her mind. Carina reached across, linking her fingers into Tia's as it calmed her enough to speak. "I thought…seeing people hurt or sick from things out of their control, like a stroke or near drowning, children falling ill…" Tia shuddered, trying not to put all of her emotions onto Carina. "Suicide. I've seen it. I've even felt it once or twice. But…" Tia looked into Carina's eyes, letting out what infuriated her most. She knew her words could come across as harsh but she was only speaking her truths. No one could understand unless they were the innocent bystanders who suffered after someone killed themselves or others.

Tia spoke as calmly as she could muster. "Enduring the outcome of it, I've realized that the person responsible for Bruce leaving us was far more selfish than a cold blooded killer. I know that sounds crazy to say but his suicidal actions affected ours, Bruce's, and his own life. It's the most selfish thing to do to another person. You don't care or think about who you'll affect. And if you do, that's worse." Tears streamed down their faces as she continued. "That guy decided he'd take someone with him. And those who witnessed it. His mom. Bruce's partner that night. The loss you and your kids have endured." Tia's voice broke, shaking her head from the misery and the anger she felt in losing Bruce. She breathed heavily through her nose and Carina handed her some tissue.

"I miss him every day." Carina lowered her head, stuck in her thoughts. "Is it wrong that I want to smile again? That I want to take the kids out for ice cream and laugh about their week in school. Hear Johnathan tell goofy made up stories and hear Michelle ask me a bunch of questions about things I have no clue about. Or Rina try to convince me that she's old enough to get a nose piercing or go to a party."

Tia considered. "No. It isn't wrong of you to want any of that. I know…Bruce would want his family to start living again."

"How do I do that?"

Tia shrugged. "Take it one day at a time."

Without warning, Carina rested her head over Tia's shoulder. "One day at a time," Carina repeated. She grunted. "Okay."

Chapter Five

Tia

"I've applied a tourniquet. It's barely working." Blood spurted out from the artery in their patient's thigh. Tia had no time to react to the blood that now resided over her clothes and neck. She pressed down harder against the thick gash over his inner thigh. The kid had gone skateboarding, leaping up on a rail. He slid a few feet atop the rail on his skateboard when he lost balance and cut himself open against a jagged edge he hadn't seen. An accident so preventable that he would die for it if they didn't gain control over his artery soon. The femoral artery was large. Many patients bled out before they had a chance to reach a hospital.

Their patient shivered, his skin pale from the lack of blood. His body was going into shock. Tia crouched over him, a puddle of blood underneath. "I'm not leaving you," Tia promised.

He looked no more than 20. Tears came out, begging for her to keep him alive. Tia squeezed his hand as hard as she could, squeezing his thigh with the same strength. "You feel that?" she whispered to her patient.

His eyes grew heavy, but he opened them wide and nodded.

"Pain means you're alive. Keep your eyes open."

"Let's move him on a count of three," her new partner for tonight said. Two fire crews went to different positions to help lift the kid. Tia kept her hand firmly against his thigh.

"I'll drive, Tia," one of the fire crew said. "Whatever you're doing, it's slowing the bleeding. We don't want to jeopardize the bleed control by removing your hand until we get to the emergency room."

Tia nodded as they entered the rig and she took a seat beside her patient. "You hear that? I'll be right here the entire time," she whispered for his ears only.

"Watch your head. I'm going to hang a saline bag over you," the fire paramedic alerted.

It took them four minutes to reach the emergency room. A trauma surgeon was right on site to clamp the artery once they arrived through the doors.

The patient was out of their care, but Tia lingered for a bit to see what they'd do next for the young man. He was scared. She could see it in his eyes and hoped he'd live. Some nights, Tia didn't want to know if her patients survived. It was better not knowing. Other nights, she had to know. Back when she had Bruce, they would decide together if they could equally handle knowing or not. Being partners for so long, they'd spoken their own language and understood what the other was feeling without words.

Tia wasn't interested in finding that with anyone else. Not that it would be easy either. An amazing partner was hard to come by. For tonight, she'd deal with working with a new temporary partner.

*

"How was your shift?" Tia's supervisor asked, coming up after she parked the ambulance into its designated spot.

"One night at a time." She had no more to say, knowing she couldn't lie but preferring not to share her sadness in the absence of Bruce.

The supervisor pointed as an SUV pulled up. "Isn't that Bruce's family?"

It was hard, hearing someone who didn't have a personal connection to Bruce say his name. Tia winced as if her supervisor had to remind her of his death. She had to look away so that her supervisor couldn't see her anguish. "Yeah. They're taking me out for pancakes."

"Oh." Tia watched as her supervisor tried to process that but then smiled. "Sounds fun."

"Yep. See you." Tia walked to the car, climbing into the front passenger seat.

Carina wore a big smile. "How was work?"

Tia twisted to find all three of Bruce's kids lying sleepily in the back seat. It was the early morning, not yet 6:30. She smiled, happy to see them. It'd been nearly a month since Tia rushed to Carina's home and this would be their first outing together since. Tia was looking forward to it. "Rough. But a kid lived at the end of the night, and that's something to treasure."

"Good." Carina pulled off, asking more questions about Tia's shift until they arrived. "Hey, you three. Wake up."

Rina whined first. "But we're sleepy. It's Saturday. I thought we could sleep in."

"Don't you want some pancakes and bacon?" Tia asked, turning to face the back.

"I do!" Johnathan opened his eyes and wiped his mouth from the slobber he'd created in his sleep.

Tia grinned. "Good to hear," she said. She looked to the center of the back seat. Michelle was still asleep. "I'll get her," she told Carina, exiting the car. The back seat had wider space, giving Tia room to climb in and carry Michelle without any trouble. Tia rocked her once and patted her back. "Hey hun, time to wake up." She bent to let Michelle stand and waited for her small sleepy eyes to open. "You want some banana pancakes? I know they're your favorite."

Michelle looked to her mom and then Tia and nodded.

"Good."

When they were seated inside the restaurant, their waitress came up and took their order. It amazed Tia how much she'd missed going out to eat. It had been so long. The last time was probably with Bruce.

Carina sat across from Tia in between Rina and Johnathan in a family sized booth. Michelle sat beside Tia, playing with one of Tia's dreadlocks that fell from her hair band.

"You sure you aren't tired?" Carina asked.

Tia smiled. "Not yet. But I will be after this meal."

Their food came in between light conversations exchanged between Tia and Carina, the kids forever silent. Tia sliced Michelle's pancakes and then began smearing butter and syrup over her own pancakes. She folded one in half and picked it up to take a bite. Eyes closed, she let the taste of deliciousness melt in her mouth. Ready for another bite, Tia felt small hands tap her shoulder. Tia looked down, finding Michelle's eyes scrutinizing her. "What? It's a taco."

Michelle smiled. A tear came to Tia's eyes instantly. It had been so long since she witnessed Michelle smile. Tia looked up to Carina, finding that she'd caught it too. They'd all missed seeing that smile, life being a little dark without it. Tia took another bite, moaning as if it was the best pancake in the world. She nodded, pleased from the taste and looked down at Michelle grinning. "The best taco ever."

It was a blessing to see Michelle giggle as she tried to cover her mouth from spitting out her pancake. She put her fork down and tapped Tia's shoulder, waving for her to come closer. Tia did, and Michelle whispered in her ear. "It's not a taco. It's a pancake."

The excitement Tia got from hearing Michelle's voice after months of silence or only her cries was overwhelming. Tia put her pancake down and stared at Michelle with such awe. She was so precious and sweet. Tia tapped Michelle's shoulder and leaned down to whisper in her small ear. "Sorry young lady, but it's a taco."

Michelle smiled and shook her head in disapproval, taking her fork to continue eating her food.

Tia looked across the table when a hand pressed over hers. She found Carina staring at her, a few tears on her face as she mouthed, *'thank you.'* A long moment of comfortable silence passed between them. When Carina removed her hand, Tia felt a sudden absence from her touch. She smiled and mouthed, *'you're welcome'* and went back to eating her folded pancake.

Chapter Six

Carina

"¿Cómo estas?" Carina's sister Sandra sat down on the bench beside her as their kids played together in the park.

Carina was the youngest of her two sisters, Sandra being the middle child and also the nosiest.

"Bien." Carina was fortunate to have such a strong support system. After losing Bruce, her family stepped up. It took so long for them to get out of the house and want to smile again. She felt her sister staring at her, as if not trusting her words. Carina smiled and patted her older sister's leg. "Estoy bien. Honesto." She was fine and needed her sister to believe that. If she did, so would their parents. Maybe they'd stop calling every day wondering when her next breakdown would be.

It was early July and officially seven months since Bruce's passing. There were times it felt like only several days had passed before Carina fell apart again. But she managed better now. She wouldn't fall apart until her kids were taken care of. That usually left her crying when she tried to sleep in their bed. Or in the shower. She'd gotten her kids into therapy and that had been working too. Not to mention, Tia being there for them in the last three months. Carina had a lot to be thankful for. There were some families that had no one after losing a loved one.

"How's work?" Sandra asked. She was being quite snoopy.

Carina smiled and rolled her eyes, knowing her sister would report everything back to their parents. She was the youngest in her family and would always be treated as such. "I work part time at the nursing home." Carina had gotten her CNA license several years back, keeping it renewed in case she ever wanted to practice again. But she liked being a stay at home mom and Bruce didn't mind working to provide financially. He would always say *she has the harder job*. "It's nice." Carina shrugged, voicing her thoughts. "I've been thinking about going to nursing school. I can't right now, but I think I want to."

"That's good." Sandra waved to her daughter, who waved back and continued playing. "The kids tell me Bruce's partner comes over a lot."

"Her name's Tia. You've met her like several dozen times." Carina rolled her eyes. Carina's family would say they weren't homophobic as long as it didn't affect their personal lives, but Carina considered them homophobic. "And yes, she comes over often. She's been such a blessing in our lives."

"I'm sure," was all Sandra said.

Carina sighed, waving her hand out. "Just say it already."

Her sister stalled for a bit, but finally gave into her impulse to judge. "Shouldn't you try and focus on the present? I only mean, Tia is kind of the past. A reminder. You'll never be able to explore new options with her around so much."

Carina winced at her sister's statement, finding every word wrong and inappropriate. Her heart raced in her chest as she attempted not to shout at her sister in a park surrounded by kids. "I lost my husband seven months ago, Sandra! I'm not interested in finding another man." Carina tried not to sound bitter, but it was unavoidable. She stared her sister down like a fighter did before a match. "And Tia is not my past. She was family before Bruce died. Is family now. With or without Bruce. And neither my children nor I blame her for staying alive." She stood, ready to take her children home.

Her sister reached out, grabbing her forearm before she sprinted to the playground. "I'm sorry, sis. I didn't mean to belittle your connection to her or imply anything. I just want what's best for you."

Carina gave a sharp nod. "I appreciate you and Miguel for all you've done since Bruce..." Carina was too sensitive now to even finish her words. She knew her sister and brother-in-law had the best intensions, but she needed to make it clear that she could be a single parent. Maybe she had been leaning on Tia too much, but she'd never try and end their friendship. "For the first time, since losing Bruce, my family feels awake again. And yes, part of that is because of Tia. She's not going anywhere. So I need you and our parents to accept that. And get over your prejudiced views."

Sandra frowned as if shocked by Carina's comment. "Come on! I never said anything about her being gay."

"You didn't have to." Carina called out to her kids. "I'll talk to you later."

*

"Can Tia come over?" Johnathan asked. "She's supposed to help me beat the next level on my game."

After the conversation with her sister at the park, Sandra's words got to Carina and she hated it. She didn't want to feel like she depended so much on Tia, but part of her did. Perhaps, that was her fault. "Honey, she might have plans or be at work."

"She's not at work, Mom. She told us she stopped working Wednesday's," Rina explained.

It was summer vacation and they had a lot of time to spare. Most of that time, they wanted to share with Tia. They'd even FaceTime her when she was at work.

"Hey guys, we should give Tia a break." Carina didn't want to smother Tia more than they already had.

"Mom, it won't hurt to ask," Rina said. It seemed she wanted Tia over too.

By the look of hope in Michelle's eyes, she felt the same.

Carina sighed. "Fine. Call and see. But don't press her if she says she can't."

"Yes!" Johnathan cheered and reached for the house phone, calling Tia.

Carina folded laundry on the couch, listening to her son talk to Tia. Based on the excited shout he made, she'd said yes. Carina smiled and continued to fold, directing her kids to take their clothes to their rooms. Carina had to admit; she was excited to see Tia too.

It took Tia 30 minutes to get there, and when she did she held a container of ice cream in one hand and bottle of wine in the other. Usually when Tia brought that combo, she wanted to talk later. It was probably a great idea.

They said hi before her kids dragged Tia off. Carina smiled, happy to know they had Tia in their lives.

After dinner and ice cream was served, the kids said their goodnights and headed upstairs. Tia worked on opening the bottle of wine while Carina grabbed two glasses. The red liquid poured into the glasses as Carina took one and swirled it. After a moment, she breathed in its sweet aroma and took a small sip. Tia loved wine. That was something Carina never knew about her in all the years she'd known her. Bruce always had a beer in hand—a regular drinker—so when Tia came over, that's what she'd drink.

"I wanted to ask for your permission." Tia pulled out an envelope, slipping out two tickets. "Uh, before, you know. Rina would try and blackmail me." Tia smiled and then cleared her throat. "She was begging me to take her to the Julia Michaels concert this summer. I never said yes, but I was always going to. It's next weekend."

Immediately, tears fell from Carina's eyes. She wiped them away as fast as they came. "You are amazing." How could she deny her kids any time spent with Tia when it was clearly what her kids and Tia needed.

Tia shook her head. "Nah, I just love your kids. They keep me going."

Everything Carina was planning to say tonight would've been wrong. Perhaps, Carina and her kids did lean on Tia a bit too much, but it was the same for her. They all needed each other. And at this moment, Carina realized they were no longer friends just because of Bruce and losing him. She reached over, squeezing Tia's hand. "You know. In the past three months, we've talked and shared things we experienced with Bruce. His leaving made us connect in a way that assures me I can trust you with my life and my kids' lives more than I ever acknowledged."

"It means a lot hearing you say that. Sometimes, I feel like I'm crowding you all up. Not giving you enough space to breathe," Tia said.

Carina laughed. "And here I thought we were doing that to you."

They both grinned and took a few sips of their wine, letting the moment soak in.

"Is it too soon to say you're my best friend?" Carina asked, feeling a bit shy about that.

Tia shook her head. "Not at all. I feel the same way."

"Good." Carina sighed in relief. "But please tell us if we're leaning on you too much. I know you haven't been out mingling with your own personal friends as much."

Tia smiled. "I'm doing better at balancing everything out. I work less. Something I never thought I'd do anytime soon."

"That's good." Carina grinned, thankful Tia was finally taking days off. She grabbed the bottle of wine and headed into the living room to take a seat. "Any potential dates?"

Tia chuckled and sat across from her on the couch. "Dates?" She rolled her eyes. "You been talking to my dad?" she jokingly asked. Tia shook her head. "No! There's no one who sparks my interest."

"But someone hot like you..." Carina snorted. Carina took a moment to admire Tia's charming wide smile and beautiful brown eyes. She had an average build, dark skinned with sloped shoulders, and thick long brown dreads free from its ponytail tonight. "I'm sure there are women who line themselves up."

"Really? You think so!?"

"Hey, I've got eyes. And even when we go out, there are women who stop and stare. Sometimes I want to give you space so I don't get in the way of a potential love connection."

Tia laughed hard, her eyes wetting with tears. "Come on. This is Oregon. They don't have enough black gay women here. Of course they're curious. Doesn't mean I'm going to go date the first, second, or third woman who approaches me."

"Wow. You must be treasure to some of these women," Carina joked.

Tia shook her head. "Being a lesbian is hard work. I make it less hard by only spending my time with those I know will be worth the time and experience."

That, Carina could understand. "I'm sure falling for another woman can have its challenges when you have so many around you that want to see you fail."

Tia nodded slowly and studied her with curiosity. "You talk as if you understand," she said.

It took Carina a moment to respond. She wondered how much she could share. "I met Bruce when I was 19. Fell in love with him instantly. And you know the rest from there." She finished her wine and poured a second glass. "But my first serious crush was when I was 16. She was my math tutor. A college student. I knew my parents would never approve of my affection for her, so I kept it to myself. I always knew I liked boys too, so I thought there was no point in having them worry about my future when I would most likely marry a man. A stupid way of thinking now that I'm older."

"What?" Tia's mouth hung open, astonished by Carina's omission. "You ever tell Bruce that?"

Carina snorted. "Yeah. He didn't care. He knew I loved him and that was enough." Carina frowned and considered. "I would've thought he told you that."

"Nah." Tia shook her head. "He never gave away anything personal about you." Tia smiled. "He loved and respected you so much."

"Yeah," Carina whispered. "He was my world." She let out a long sigh. "Wait right here." Carina got up, rushing up the stairs and came back down with some paperwork. She opened the large manila envelope, pulling out documents. "I never showed this to you because I didn't want to put this kind of pressure on you, but I realize now I was wrong in not sharing this with you." Carina handed it over to Tia to read.

Tia looked wryly at Carina but stared down, reading the first page. "What is this?"

Carina pointed to the paperwork at the top. "It's our will. He never got around to asking you, but we both agreed that if we both passed, we'd name you acting guardian over our children."

Tia's eyes lifted so fast. Her body jolted, nearly spilling her wine. She placed it on the end table and continued to read.

"He had no siblings. His parents are too strict; he'd never wish the hard life he had with them on his kids. My sisters have enough responsibilities of their own and my parents… it just wouldn't work. One thing is clear. We wanted you to be a permanent member in our family's lives. And the only way to make sure that happened was to name you as their guardian."

"I—I don't know what to say."

"Well…I'm still here so that leaves us with the second will he made."

Tia flipped through the pages to find the second one.

"The second one states that he wanted you to be the guardian angel over his family." Carina snorted. "His exact words."

Tia laughed. "Guardian angel." She looked to Carina, searching her eyes for any signs of sadness or anger from the will.

"He asks you to do and be who you've been for us in the last three months. Someone we can lean on. But he forgot one thing."

"What's that?"

"That we should be that for you too. And we do cherish the times you've leaned on us, even though you try not to."

Tia closed her eyes and smiled. "Thank you for showing me this. I don't ever want to let you guys down again."

Carina waved out her hand. "Please don't. You needed to grieve in your own way. You're here now."

"Best friends," Tia said, holding out her glass.

The peace in knowing Tia would always be around... Carina leaned forward, clicking their glasses together. "Best friends."

Chapter Seven

Carina

Carina heard the front door open and watched as Rina rushed to her in excitement.

"Mom! It was so much fun. Julia Michaels was like 30 feet from us. And Tia got us VIP passes to the backstage. Look." Rina came up, leaping onto the couch with a photo in hand. "See!"

Carina chuckled. "I see, sweetie."

One by one, Rina showed her mom pictures and videos of the concert. It would be days before Rina finally calmed down about the concert and could be excited for something new.

It was late. Rina eventually went upstairs for bed, giving Tia one last hug.

Tia smiled at Carina, pointing off toward the front door. She looked exhausted. "I should get going."

"It's late. I can tell my daughter took all your energy. Stay the night."

"I don't want to—"

"You don't want to what? Cramp my style? Overstay your welcome?" Carina shrugged. "Stay. The couch is always yours to take."

"Thanks."

"I'll get you some blankets." Carina stood and headed upstairs. She found Rina still looking through her phone and walked in. She sat on the bed beside her daughter. "You tell Tia thank you?"

"Yeah, Mom," Rina muttered, distracted with the pictures in her phone. She hadn't looked up since Carina walked in.

Carina bumped her shoulder into her daughter's. "Hey. We're fortunate to have her. Please make sure you show her how much you appreciate her."

"Mom." Rina put the phone down, finally making eye-contact. "I did! I told her that I'm happy dad brought her into our life. And sorry for the time I was mad at her."

"That was mature of you." She kissed her daughter's forehead. "Get some sleep. It's late."

"K, Mom."

Carina headed back downstairs with two blankets finding Tia asleep stretched out on the couch, one foot rested on the floor. Her dreads were freed from its hair band. She looked so peaceful Carina didn't want to disturb her resting body. Carina took one of the blankets and spread it over Tia. She knelt beside her, removing the sunglasses dangled around her necklace. Without thinking, Carina brushed her knuckles over Tia's cheek. Carina stood, thankful to have Tia in her life.

*

Tia

"Thanks for letting me stay the night." Tia put on her shoes, ready to head out. After passing out on the couch, Tia woke up the next morning with the kids running around.

"You should come with us," Carina blurted out. For some reason, she wasn't ready to see Tia leave.

"Go with you to your family picnic?" Tia asked slowly, as if unsure of what Carina was referring to. "With your parents, sisters, and their families. Cousins."

Carina laughed. "When you say it like that... I know they're difficult. I'm sorry. I realize how stupid it was of me to say that."

"Hey. Stupid is not a word to use," Tia said and sighed. "Honestly, I'm not worried about them. Only that they'll probably give you a hard time for inviting me."

Carina nodded, understanding what Tia didn't say aloud. Her family didn't care about Tia's sexuality until they began hanging out together. "I know the kids would be excited if you came. I just know I want you there. You're family to us too." Carina looked away, feeling a bit vulnerable. She didn't know why she suddenly felt nervous around Tia and tried to hide it.

"Okay. I'll come. I should get home and change. You can send me the address."

"I'll do that." Carina smiled and watched Tia leave wondering to herself what she was thinking inviting Tia to face her family after Sandra's comments several days ago. There was no turning back now and Carina didn't want to.

*

Carina

"Papa." Carina gave her father a kiss on the cheek. "I've missed you."

"¿Cómo está mi chica?"

Carina smiled to her father. "I'm good, Papa." She sat beside him at the picnic table, taking a tamale from the basket. "The kids are happy to see everyone."

"You happy?" he asked with an overly curious expression plastered over his face.

"Happier than I was last month," she stated. She blocked out the thoughts that triggered her tears. She smiled, attempting to be strong.

"Bueno." Her father nodded then called to Johnathan, asking him to come over. "How's my young man? Are you protecting your mother?"

"Yes, Grandpa," Johnathan said. "We all protect Mom. Including Tia."

"Tia?" Her father's tone held curiosity. Carina sighed, seeing her father's eyes perk up.

"Yeah. She's coming too," Johnathan smiled. "Can I go play with Carlos and Tony?"

"Go on, sweetie." Carina addressed her son. When he ran off, Carina waited to hear her father make his first disapproval of the day.

The silence lasted longer than expected until her father grumbled in Spanish under his breath. He gave Carina a long look before speaking."¿Qué estás haciendo?"

"What do you mean?" Carina asked as if oblivious by his inquisition.

"You spend too much time with this woman," he argued, waving his hand frantically.

As suspected, her sister Sandra had been feeding her parents intel. Carina scowled. "She's my friend. What's wrong with spending time together?"

"Too much time," her father retorted. "And then you invite her to a family gathering."

Carina didn't come here to get lectured. She looked up, hearing her kids shout Tia's name. "Papa, you can think what you want. But for me and my kids, she is family." Carina stood and walked toward Tia.

They met up near the long table where all the food resided. "Hungry?" Carina asked, pretending like her father hadn't just disapproved of her relationship with Tia. She reached in for a hug and Tia accepted it.

"Starved." They made a plate of food and sat alone at a table. Tia glanced around. "Looks like most of your family are happy to see me."

"I'm happy to see you. That should count." Carina smiled, their eyes locking for some time. There was something different about Tia that gave Carina the impulse to always want to be near her. She felt most happy when Tia was around. It was no longer about the reminder of Bruce through the stories Tia shared. It was just Tia being Tia.

"It counts," Tia said softly. She smiled and looked away.

"Hi! You must be the famous Tia." Carina's older cousin, Tomas, offered his hand and sat down with his wife at his side.

They introduced themselves to Tia making her feel welcomed. Carina was thankful for the few relatives she had that genuinely wanted to know Tia. They talked for some time, Tia and Tomas debating about the best movies currently out, when Carina was waved over by both of her sisters and her mom.

She dismissed herself from Tomas and Tia's conversation, promising to come back. "We thought you'd never tear yourself away from her," Sandra joked, no humor in her voice.

"Sandra, don't be an ass too," Carina's other sister Gina stated. Carina smiled to her eldest sister Gina, thankful to have her support.

Carina frowned and didn't bother walking any closer, standing a few feet from them. "If you're going to start this, I'm turning around."

"Your sister means well," her mother said. Her mother's Spanish accent was thick, English being her second language. Gina gave Carina a hug before heading over to her husband.

Carina walked the rest of the way over to her mom and gave her a hug and a kiss. "I really need you both to respect my choices and who I allow into my kids' lives."

"Honey. We aren't worried about your kids with her. We can tell she adores them and they her. It's you we're concerned for." Her sister Sandra gave a cautious smile.

"What does that even mean?" Carina couldn't fathom why they were making such a big deal out of this.

"You care for her," Sandra said almost accusatory.

"Of course I do." Carina stared dumbfounded.

"A bit too much." Her sister added, waving her arms frantically like her father. Sandra stared at her as if Carina was supposed to understand what she was trying to say.

Carina snorted, finding this conversation ridiculous. "What are you talking about?"

"Maybe you don't see it because you aren't ready to." Sandra sighed.

"See what?" Carina said a bit too loud. A few of her family heard her yell and looked up. Tia looked to her, making sure she was okay. Carina smiled and nodded. Their eyes locked for a few seconds and Carina relaxed.

When she turned back to her mom and sister, their eyes held scrutiny.

"That, honey! What you just did is our point. She's confusing you. You spend too much time with her." Her mom spoke as if she needed saving.

"Tia doesn't confuse me. The only people confusing me are the two of you."

"The way you talk about her. The way I caught you looking at her earlier." This time her sister didn't hold back, wanting to make her point. "You like her. And maybe because you aren't ready to see that—which is a good thing—you don't realize it. But I do know, if you don't put distance between you two soon, you'll see what we mean and it'll destroy your friendship with her."

Carina frowned and looked to Tia. She couldn't imagine losing her as a friend. But she couldn't allow her family to dictate who she should be close to. There was nothing between her and Tia except friendship. She wouldn't ruin that out of fear. "I appreciate your concern. Both of you. But I'm fine." She turned and headed back to Tia.

It took her a minute to look up, Tia studying her wry eyes. Carina found the courage and faced her with a sincere smile. Her family was being dramatic like always. There was no doubt she cared about Tia, but not in the way they described.

"You okay?" Tia asked.

"I will be."

*

"You sure you're okay?" Tia asked for the fifth time. They were back at Carina's house. She helped put the leftover food away in the fridge as the kids slugged their way up the stairs. All that excitement tired them out.

Carina stared off, lost in her thoughts. A hand brushed her arm and she jumped back, startled. "Oh, I guess I'm tired."Carina regretted the words the moment she spoke them. She was nowhere near tired and wanted to spend more time with Tia without her kids interrupting them, but fear got the best of her.

Tia smiled. "Okay. I get the hint." She put the last of the food away and said goodbye, heading out of the house doing her best not to appear disappointed.

In regret, Carina sighed, covering her face with shame. She'd let her mom and sister's words get to her. No matter how much she defended her relationship with Tia to them she was being a hypocrite now. "Way to go," she told herself and headed upstairs.

Alone in her room, Carina had nothing but time to think about everything. What her sister and her mom implied… Carina couldn't allow her thoughts to go there. It would be foolish and naive to even try. They were wrong.

In need of a shower, Carina opened the drawer to pull out clean clothes. She stopped and walked over to the second dresser where all of Bruce's clothes were. She hadn't found the courage to pack his things. Had it been too long? Over seven months since his passing and she couldn't let him go. Her hands shook as she opened the drawer. It was a collection of his tank tops and briefs. Carina ran her hands over his things.

In grief, she slammed the dresser shut, turning her back to it. She hated being without him and wanted to bury herself in his belongings. Part of her knew she needed to move on, but the other half wasn't ready. It was too soon.

Carina took a long breath and whispered the words Tia gave her. "One day at a time."

Chapter Eight

Tia

"Tia. You haven't found a decent partner yet. And it's not because people don't like working your shift. You're not giving anyone a chance." Her supervisor had called her in before her shift started.

Instead of listening to her supervisor, Tia listened to the wind blow harshly as rain fell from the sky. It was a terribly cold night to be working. Nearly Halloween, she and Bruce would normally decorate their ambulance.

"It's been 10 months. Perhaps, you should have another extended holiday vacation. You have more than enough PTO. Take it."

Tia nodded. "I'll consider it."

Her supervisor sighed and leaned back into his seat. "This paramedic you're working with has served two tours as a combat medic. Just got back into the states. He's experienced and downright funny. I think you two have a lot in common. Give him a chance."

Tia smiled, saying nothing more. She stood. "Can I get to work?"

"Go on."

Headed to her rig, Tia didn't bother making conversation with anyone. They all knew not to try. She wanted it that way.

It seemed they found her a permanent partner. I'm sure the supervisors warned him about her, so she was a bit curious as to why he'd agreed so easily to be her partner.

She opened the back rig, finding a man who appeared to be in his mid 30s. He was tall, with blonde hair and green eyes. He smiled and offered his hand. "I'm Joe Burton. You must be Benson."

Tia studied his hand for a time, wondering if she should even try. Her contemplating took too long, and he pulled his hand away.

He smiled. "I get it. I look creepy."

Tia frowned, confused by his statement. She gave him a second glance, trying to figure out what the hell made him look creepy. She was about to dismiss him altogether when she noticed a scar hikcd up the side of his neck to the end of his jaw. It was almost an inch thick and who knew how long. The bottom half of his scar hid underneath his shirt.

Instead of acknowledging his scar, Tia climbed in and began going over their supplies. Even the ones he'd already went over. He seemed unbothered by her task of checking over his work. After several minutes of making sure they had all they needed, Tia climbed into the driver's seat, checking all their lights and sirens.

He climbed in and put on his seatbelt. He didn't bother trying to reach for the mic or ask her anything else, he simply looked forward and waited.

Dispatch sounded over the intercom, giving another ambulance unit a call when she picked up the mic. They were the only ambulance left without a call. It was a busy night. "This is Medic 111 to Dispatch, we are on the air and ready for a post."

A few seconds rolled by when a call popped off.

"This is dispatch to Medic 111…" The dispatch gave them the address and Tia turned on her lights and sirens knowing that at 6pm they'd have rush hour to get through. It was dark out as the blue and red lights turned on.

It was a call to a possible overdose in a vehicle parked at a grocery store. It took them seven minutes to arrive and they were first on scene. Tia put on her gloves, grabbing the gurney and airway bag. She walked up to the truck, knocking hard on the window. There was a man inside. He didn't move, his head draped to one side.

"The door's locked," she told Joe, going around to the back passenger side door. "All the doors are locked." She pulled out a tactical pen that could shatter glass. "I'm going to smash his back window in."

"Sounds good," he didn't argue.

Tia took a step back and used the tip of her tactical pen as it slammed against the window and shattered it. Tia wasted no time, being careful as she reached over and unlocked the door, twisting her arm further inside and unlocking the front passenger door. Thankfully she wore protective eye gear; a few glass pieces hit her chin. She moved around to open the front door and pressed the control to unlock all the doors.

Joe opened the door to where the man sat unconscious, taking abnormal, high-pitched breaths every several seconds. He pulled the patient forward, pressing him into the steering wheel to check his back for dirty needles. Tia checked his sides. She looked down at the floor of the driver's seat and grimaced, pointing out calmly. "Gun."

He followed her line of sight, flinging the man forward and carefully reaching for the gun to place it under the car on the ground. "Cleared," he shouted.

"Needle between his legs," Tia called out.

"Damn, you have good eyes. Copy," Joe said, complimenting her as he removed the dirty needle.

Their safety came first. Now that they had everything cleared, it was time to work to save their patient. The fire truck pulled up—one paramedic—assisting them to extricate their patient out of the truck and plant him on the gurney. The patient's hand jerked up and smacked the paramedic in the face.

"Damn it." The fire paramedic worked to remove his shirt and cut his pants legs open.

Tia went for the airway bag, pulling out a King airway tube. "I'm going straight to a King tube," Tia announced. She made sure the balloon was deflated, tilting his head back and slid the thick tube down his throat. There was no gag reflex, which would make this easy. Once placed inside, she inflated the balloon and attached the bag-valve to it, forcing air into his lungs with every breath he attempted to make.

He was a big guy. He took another breath as she forced more air into his lungs. "Restrain him," she ordered.

The fire paramedic frowned, shaking his head. "There's no need. He won't be able to do anything with all of us over him."

"No disrespect, but this is my ambulance at the end of the day. I want him restrained." There was a time Tia wouldn't have made a big deal about it. But after losing her partner to a patient, one who appeared violent at the time, Tia had a hard time trusting her own patient's intensions. She'd found this man with a gun and he might wake up irrational. She needed to have him restrained.

"My partner says restrain him. We do that," Joe agreed. He locked eyes with Tia and went back to attaching him to the cardiac monitor. The fire crew worked to restrain his ankles and wrists.

"I'm going to give him Narcan," Joe said.

Once administered, it took their patient a few minutes before it kicked in. He snapped his head to one side, shaking his arms to get free. His eyes rolled back. He was better with the Narcan but not out of the danger zone. His saturation was still low, and he still needed assistance breathing.

"I'll get us to the hospital in five." Tia hopped out the back and went to the driver seat, ready to take off. It took her exactly five minutes to get to the hospital.

There was no time for breaks. As soon as they cleared one call another popped up. It seemed like they were the shit magnets for tonight.

By the end of their shift, Tia pulled into the ambulance bay, ready to take a nap in the back of the rig. They'd been running call after call with no breaks.

"Well…seems I took the calm out of your shift tonight," Joe joked.

Tia nodded, and turned off the rig. She was about to open the door when Joe sighed as if something was on his mind. "Yeah." She looked to him, waiting for him to tell her she was rude or something along those lines.

"My first tour lasted 13 months. I had a whole unit I worked with. Out of those 13 months, the first 10 were the best because I had my best friend beside me. Until we were gunned down and trapped in a building for 27 hours. And for 20 of those hours, I sat beside my best friend with a bullet lodged in his head."

It took Tia a minute to process that. She eventually acknowledged him, finding pain in his eyes. He was opening up to her and she hadn't even tried with him. Her supervisor was not kidding when he said they'd have a lot in common.

"I know and understand what it's like to lose your partner. The person who understood you better than anyone, could read your thoughts. Know when you needed to take a shit. Someone you trusted with your life. My last tour, the combat medic I had to work beside…" He chuckled. "I didn't want to know her. Get close to her. But I had no choice. It's life or death. I either do it alone, or open up and hope she's worth trusting. Hope I don't lose her too."

In the back of Tia's mind, that had been her second greatest fear. That she'd trust someone new and lose them too. She took in a long breath, fighting back to urge to cry.

"Honestly…during my orientation here, when people told me about you and the partner you lost, I asked for you." Tia shifted a glance his way, shocked and curious. He smiled. "I figured if anyone would take this job seriously, it would be you. You carry so much pain for the person you lost. I thought you'd understand me and the decisions I'd have to make on calls we go on. Decisions you'd make with me. And when you finally opened up, you'd have my back and I'd have yours."

Joe smiled. "I'm not expecting you to share your past with me and call me a friend tomorrow. I just hope that you can try." He opened the door. "Have a good night!"

Tia sat in the rig for some time, thinking about all that he said. The sun was barely coming out. For people who worked through the night, morning was their bedtime. Tia had to admit he was cool and knew what he was doing. There were even moments they worked where they flowed together without much being said. He was competent. Bruce would like him and tell her to give him a chance.

There was no point in deciding now. She was tired and needed to find a bed, or for her, a couch. She'd think later.

*

"How was your shift?" Tia woke up to her dad eating a bowl of rice on the small sofa next to the one she slept on. He had the TV volume on low, but his chewing woke her up. She really needed to find a place to live.

Tia had given up her apartment to save money and help Carina with bills and other things. Carina never took her money, but allowed for her to buy groceries and other things.

The last few months had been up and down between them. Something had changed for Carina and she was trying to maintain some emotional distance. Tia suspected it had to do with the family picnic she went to a couple months back.

She saw the kids about once a week, but even less of Carina. They talked on the phone, but it wasn't the same thing.

Tia sat up. "It was okay." She didn't want to get into the shift she had or her new partner. She checked her phone, finding a missed call from one of her friends, Jayden, whom she hadn't seen in a month.

After showering, Tia found a text from that old friend and they agreed to go out for drinks. She met up with Jayden, finding her flirting with a girl sitting at the bar.

"I can go home and back to sleep if you want," Tia joked.

Jayden rolled her eyes and turned to give her a hug. "I was just talking to this lovely date of mine."

"Date?" Tia frowned, confused.

"Hi, I'm Janet."

Tia gave her friend a suspicious look but shook the woman's hand. "Did you text me just so I could be your third wheel?" Tia asked.

"No," Jayden said slowly. She smiled cheekily and pointed to the booth. "I thought, well, Janet's roommate needed to get out and I thought, why not hit you up and all four of us come out and socialize."

"Just to be clear, I warned her this was a bad idea," Janet explained.

Tia looked to the direction Jayden had pointed to, finding a woman sitting alone staring at her phone. She had brunette hair with a round face. She looked elegant from the light makeup she wore to her colorful clothes. She was full figured and looked well defined for her.

Jayden clapped her hands once. "I knew you'd like her," she said, pulling her date back to the table.

Here she was on a blind date. Tia decided to go along with it and headed over. She introduced herself, finding out her name. Bailey.

"Tia's an EMT," Jayden bragged.

"I'm sure they don't want to hear that," Tia chastised. She didn't like for people to know. Then the questions would come up, asking about her worst calls. No one really ever wanted to hear the truth about the worst calls. Only the funny ones. Since losing Bruce, it was even harder for Tia to share anything about her job.

Bailey smiled. "I knew you looked familiar."

Tia looked up, confused.

Bailey smiled awkwardly. "God. You're the one who lost your partner."

All light left Tia's eyes from the mention of Bruce. Tia said nothing, picking up her drink to distance herself emotionally.

"I'm an RN. I work in the intensive care unit at Unity. That night, I was working as a resource nurse and they needed helping hands in the ER. I worked on your partner."

Out of all the people to meet, Tia couldn't take this right now. She stood, pulling out a 10. "I've got to go." She rushed out.

She felt utterly alone and heartbroken. She wasn't ready to let go of Bruce. Every time she tried, something or someone else always pulled her back in. Tia didn't want to go home. It was after 10. She considered going to the gym but didn't have her workout clothes. She sat in her car for some time until making a choice.

The rain came down hard as she pulled up to Carina's house. She texted her to see if she was home. Carina texted back and told her she was outside.

She climbed out of the car and rushed to the porch, hoping Carina would come down and open it. There had been distance between them, but she knew Carina cared about her.

The porch light turned on and the door opened. Tia spoke before Carina had the chance to. "I get that I'm probably a reminder of Bruce and you can't be around me as much anymore. But you said I needed you too. And I do." Tears fell from her eyes as she felt every part of grief slam into her chest and twist her stomach into tight knots.

Carina pulled her inside and into a hug. Tia stood a few inches taller, bending her head down to rest over Carina's shoulder.

She cried for some time, glued to Carina until exhaustion swept over her. Carina guided her into the living room. The fireplace was on. There was a book and a blanket on the couch.

Tia noticed a filled cup and light music playing. "I'm sorry. I didn't mean to interrupt your night. I can go."

"Nonsense." Carina pointed to the couch. "Sit. I'll get you some hot chocolate."

Tia nodded and went to the couch, removing her shoes and coat. Her hair was wet from the rain and she let it out of the bun, her dreads free around her shoulders and back.

A few minutes of listening to orchestra music in the background brought her some peace. She watched Carina walk around the couch, handing her a mug of hot chocolate. "Who's playing?" Tia asked.

Carina blushed, as if being caught playing something inappropriate. "It's the *Lord of the Rings* soundtrack."

A smile lifted a bit of the sadness from her bruised heart. She adored the uniqueness in Carina. It was evident Carina was taking the night for herself. "I didn't mean—" Tia paused and gave up on lying. "I had a long shift. And then after what I just experienced in the last hour, I needed you to tell me it was all okay."

Afraid to watch for a reaction, Tia let the warmth of the hot chocolate sooth her. The music did have that fantasy world vibe as she continued to listen to it. It was something new she learned about Carina that made her smile.

Ready to face Carina's honesty, Tia searched her eyes as she spoke. "Did I do something wrong?"

Carina's eyes widened. She sighed and smiled weakly. "No." She couldn't maintain eye contact.

"But something happened," Tia pushed. "Every time I come to see the kids or take them for ice cream, you're always busy. I don't just come for them, you know. You mean a lot to me too."

"I know," Carina said, feeling defeated. It looked like she had a lot on her mind. "I should've been honest with you." Carina used the remote to turn down the music. She shifted on the couch to give Tia her full attention. "You've been more than I expected. Like a second parent to my kids. And that's been great…"

"But not what you need," Tia finished.

Carina nodded. "No one could ever replace Bruce. And I know that's not what you were trying to do. But in a way, maybe I was. I needed to take a step back and evaluate things."

"And basically cutting me out is the way to do it?" Tia asked. She was hurt, and now wondering if it was really a good idea to come here. "I'm so stupid." Tia put the mug on the end table, about to stand.

Carina slid over quickly, putting her hand on Tia's thigh. "First. So not cool. You're not stupid. You can't use a word you dislike on yourself." She kept her hand on Tia's thigh. It took Tia a second to focus. "Second. I'm the one who was foolish. I've been very jealous of my kids the last couple months. Wishing I was with you. With you all," she quickly added. She stumbled over her words, suddenly looking nervous.

She removed her hand from Tia's thigh and an absence was felt, coldness sweeping over Tia's flesh. She didn't want to go there in her mind, and she wouldn't.

"I've been such a coward, wanting to call you," Carina said.

"Seems I beat you to it," Tia joked.

"Seems so."

They both smiled and relaxed for the first time tonight. After the hard part of the conversation was over, they began to discuss what they'd been up to, conversation moving into a much more intimate discussion.

"So, your friend set you up on a blind double date. But you decided to come here and ditch them." Carina snorted. "She must've been really bad for you to ditch her for me."

"Actually, she wasn't," Tia admitted. She took her time, wondering if she should tell her why she left and decided on the truth. When she finished telling Carina, she saw sadness pass through her eyes. "Yeah. So, you can see why I ran out. I feel so rude."

"She'll understand," Carina said, sounding strong.

Tia half expected her to break down from what she'd shared.

"I finally cleared out most of Bruce's things from my room a month ago. Gave a few things to the kids, and the rest I donated."

"Really?" Tia smiled, proud of Carina for facing that hardship and surviving it.

"I wish I was as strong as you. I've treated every paramedic I've worked with like the plague. I just get so angry, not seeing him sit beside me." Tia pursed her lips, thinking about her new partner. "This new guy went through a hard experience too. That's putting it mildly. But he lost his partner. I want to give him a chance. But then, I'm afraid Bruce will disappear from everyone's memories back at the station. Disappear from mine."

"He'll never disappear," Carina promised. She smiled. "You should try and go out with that woman. And give that partner a chance. Try a lot of things."

Tia shook her head. "No. She seemed sweet. But not someone I want. And I'll consider the new partner."

"What kind of woman would you want?"

That question seemed to make Tia blush. She lowered her head, covering her face with her hand.

Carina laughed. "Are you going shy on me?"

Tia rolled her eyes. "I'm not shy. I just—I feel like I've seen it all. I know what I need and when I find that woman, I only hope she loves me back."

Silence fell between them. Tia could feel Carina's gaze, and she took a chance, looking up. Their eyes locked. Tia's heart beat fast in her chest, swept away by the dark brown of Carina's irises. Neither seemed bothered by the silence.

Carina's phone rang and she jumped. "Saved by the bell," she mumbled, taking a breath. Carina looked away and reached for her phone, answering it.

Tia turned away, pulling out her phone to text her friend she was okay. She'd have to make it up to her for running out like that. For now, she was thankful for whoever called Carina this late. They'd been talking for over an hour. That moment of silence pulled out a lot of tension that clearly Carina felt too.

Carina hung up. "The kids are over at my sister's. They'll be back tomorrow." Her skin appeared flushed, and she couldn't seem to maintain eye contact for too long.

They were alone. Tia felt nervous about that too. "It's late. I don't want to keep you up."

"Right," Carina said. She frowned and shook her head. "No, wait! We're friends. And I don't want to kick you out. Especially the way it's raining right now. I'm not tired."

"Are you sure?" Tia asked.

"Yes."

Tia excused herself, needing to use the restroom. When she finished, she turned on the faucet, running cold water over her hands. What was going on with her? Maybe she just missed Carina too much. Tia preached repeatedly that what she was feeling wasn't real. Tia studied herself in the mirror. She'd always struggled with her weight, being a few pounds over since Bruce's passing. Tia was still in shape and that's what mattered. She needed to stop being so hard on herself. "Stop analyzing yourself. There's no one you need to impress. She is your best friend's wife." *Was.* Bruce was gone, but that left no excuses. Tia splashed cold water over her face and dripped more down her shirt. She needed to get a grip.

Back in the living room, Carina held a bottle of wine in her hand, holding it up to show what kind of night to expect.

Tia smiled, knowing this would be a long night, not forgotten.

Chapter Nine

Carina

The weight of someone's body kept Carina planted as she opened her eyes. The front door slammed shut, a multitude of footsteps coming her way. Carina looked over at the floor where an empty bottle of wine lay. She reached out, realizing her fingers were tangled in something. Someone's breath tickled her exposed belly and she shuddered from not feeling someone that close to her in months.

"Mom!" Rina's eyes widened and then she shouted in bliss. "Tia! You're here."

By the sound of her name, Tia's head shot up but quickly jerked back down.

Carina realized her fingers were tangled in Tia's hair.

The rest of her kids entered the living room, unsure of what to make of the situation.

"Hey, Carina!" Sandra stopped, her mouth agape as if she'd walked in on Carina in a compromising position. "Um, kids, go put your stuff away," Sandra ordered.

Tia slid off Carina, wiping the sleep from her eyes.

"Tia. Could you give my sister and me a moment?" Sandra asked.

There was no way she'd let her sister come and dictate anyone in her house. "No! Tia is fine right here."

"You really want to have this conversation in front of her?" Sandra asked.

"I prefer not at all," Carina admitted.

"Perhaps I should go home," Tia butted in.

"No!" Carina said.

"Sounds like a good idea," Sandra argued.

Tia stood, not wanting to get in between a family argument. She only grew up with her dad, but she had a suspicion that when it came to two sisters it was best to step back.

"Please don't go," Carina said.

How could Tia say no to that? She sighed. "I'll wait upstairs."

Carina nodded. She watched Tia leave until she could no longer see her and then faced her sister.

"I thought you distanced yourself from her?" Her sister asked with a hot temper ready to spill out.

"I did. But last night—no! I'm not going to explain myself to you. Tia's my friend."

"Friend!" Sandra snorted, bemused. "Is what we just walked in on? A friendly thing?"

"Nothing happened, Sandra. We were drinking and talking and then passed out." Carina shrugged. "I don't see the harm."

"Your kids are who you're harming!" Sandra shouted. She blew out a breath and shook her head. "Maybe nothing happened. But to them, it seemed that way, at least for Rina. How do you think your kids would handle knowing their mom is hooking up with their dad's old best friend who's a woman? Sorry sis, but that's a jump."

Carina's eyes hardened. She could deal with a lot of things, but being questioned as a mother was one thing she couldn't let pass. "You know, there are a lot of things kids have to endure because of their parents. But I've taught mine to value themselves and as long as things are done with a pure heart and out of love, things will be all right. My kids are not homophobic, and they understand how important Tia is to us." Carina stepped closer, lowering her voice. "Nothing happened between Tia and me. But if I ever decided to be with a woman or Tia, which as I've stated before, I'm not ready to be with anyone, I'll talk to my kids about it personally so they know how I feel and what they feel too."

"So, you're saying you'd consider being with her?" Out of all Carina had said that's all her sister heard.

"You're so into this woman and you don't even know it." Sandra shook her head and walked off. "Fine. I'm done trying to tell you anything."

Carina heard the front door shut and closed her eyes. She heard someone coming downstairs and knew Tia was approaching.

"She's why you put distance between us? Because she thinks I'm influencing you?" Tia sounded hurt.

Carina didn't want to end up arguing with Tia too. "What I told you last night is true," she defended.

"But not all true," Tia retorted. Carina said nothing and that answer was enough. Tia shook her head. The idea that they were having this compromising conversation was unsettling. Tia felt something with Carina she shouldn't have, and it needed to end. "You know, I'd never do anything to disrespect you or Bruce. Maybe coming here last night was a mistake. Because if anything, for the first time, I feel like I insulted his memories. They shouldn't have found us like that."

"Tia," Carina called out as Tia turned to leave, headed for the front door. "Please!" They stood close, the

83

front door in view. Carina pinched the bridge of her nose, a migraine from her mild hangover making its first appearance. "Why do you always try to leave when no one's trying to kick you out? It's like you're trying to spare yourself."

Tia waved her hands out, not knowing where to put them. A complication like this could ruin their friendship and Tia couldn't imagine life without Carina and her kids. "I don't ever want to do anything that would dishonor Bruce and the friendship we had."

"You could never dishonor him, Tia. Neither could I nor my kids." Carina reached for her hand, but Tia pulled back.

"I can't."

Carina wanted so badly for Tia to stop fearing the connection they had and just be emotionally present. "Tia, I'm not contemplating being with someone else in that kind of way. I'm barely emptying the house of Bruce's things. I'm not ready for that." Carina's eyes teared up, trying to get Tia to see the truth. "I just like being near you." Her voice softened almost to a whisper, vulnerable enough to share her thoughts. "You make me feel safe. And strong. I like knowing you can lean on me too. I missed you. Neither of us is doing anything wrong. And I'm not asking you to stay because you remind me of Bruce in some twisted way. I'm sorry, but you don't look or act like him." Carina smiled. "I like having you around. I tried the *not having you around* thing, and that didn't work out for you nor me. We're friends. That's all I want and need from you."

Tia cracked her knuckles, unsure what to think or believe.

Carina stepped forward, linking their fingers together. It amazed Carina how soft Tia's hands were, how she never wanted to let go. "We need each other."

Tia nodded. "Okay."

*

Carina

Tia went home and it was now time to face the music. She called her kids down wanting to talk to them. She hadn't meant for them to walk in with Tia and her asleep together. But she needed to be responsible and own up to what they saw, listen to their thoughts.

"So…you guys didn't expect to see Tia here, huh?" Carina was nervous to have this conversation. She hadn't processed what happened last night. Tia and her had been talking and drinking, eventually falling asleep. Carina wasn't someone who fell asleep with just anyone.

"Well no!" Johnathan said. "We know auntie made you feel bad for being Tia's friend. We have ears," he exaggerated, pointing to his.

"Your auntie means well. She's just use to a certain way," Carina explained.

"Is it because Tia's a lesbian?" Rina asked.

Carina smiled. She had to remind herself Rina was now 12 and growing. The only person who looked confused by the word was Michelle.

"Lesbian?" Michelle looked up to her sister for an explanation, wearing a frown.

"It means she likes going out with other girls." Johnathan took the lead on that.

"Come. Sit." Carina let Michelle sit on her lap, while Rina and Johnathan sat on the couch beside her ready to listen. "Sometimes, people don't know how to accept someone different from them. And it scares them."

"Like Auntie Sandra?" Michelle asked.

"Exactly." Carina smiled, knowing that was the easiest part to explain.

"Aunt Sandra thinks Tia can make you a lesbian?" Rina questioned.

Carina pursed her lips, knowing this conversation might not go as easily as she expected. "No one can turn someone into a lesbian. You can…help someone discover themselves and realize they like dating someone different than what they're use to."

"So, Tia helped you discover you like girls?" Johnathan asked, looking confused by his own question.

Carina shook her head. "Honey. What you guys walked in on was purely innocent. We had a sleep over." There was nothing more between Tia and her than friendship. Carina couldn't picture being with anyone.

"I have sleepovers too, Mom. That didn't look like a normal sleepover," Rina objected.

"Tia and I are only friends, honey. I promise you. If I ever felt ready to be with anyone, I'd let you guys know."

"And if it's Tia?" Rina asked.

Carina was about to say it never would be, but that felt like a lie. She didn't know what she truly felt, but when she was ready to feel for someone other than her husband, she'd figure it out. "Honey, right now, it's no one. I do hope you three don't treat Tia differently for what happened this morning."

"We won't, Mom," Rina said. She looked uncomfortable.

"But, I don't get why she doesn't like Tia." Michelle shrugged her little shoulders. "Everyone loves Tia. Daddy loved Tia."

Carina was grateful to have open minded kids. She kissed Michelle's cheek. "As long as we love Tia, that's what matters." Her daughter was talking again and that was because of Tia. Whatever was happening between her and Tia, there was no need to define it. Carina had a lot to work on and she still thought of Bruce every day. She might never let a day pass without thinking of him.

*

"Mrs. Simpson."

Carina turned, finding the supervisor of the station approaching. She smiled and waved, being polite. Bruce had gone out for drinks with the guy a few times. It was a little after 5:30pm, the sky darkening.

"Did you need something?" he asked.

An ambulance pulled out of the garage, freshly washed and dripping water, and Carina searched for Tia in the driver's seat. It was a man parking it out front of the ambulance bay.

Carina pointed to the ambulance. "I came to see Tia," she clarified.

"Oh." He smiled, looking off toward the garage. "Here she comes now." His puzzled expression didn't go unnoticed. "Have a good night, Mrs. Simpson."

He'd said her last name as if to remind her of who she was and who she belonged to. Carina smirked, finding it exhausting how so many people found it weird for her and Tia to be so close, as if she was supposed to end their connection the moment Bruce died.

Carina walked to the ambulance, knocking on the door and opening it. Tia sat inside, going through her phone. "So...you didn't lose it?" Carina shook her head, disappointed, and climbed in. "For someone who says she doesn't want to lose us, you sure do know how to disappear."

"Carina, I—"

Not in the mood to hear an excuse, Carina lifted her hand. "Don't." She took in all the supplies they carried in the back of the rig. She could never understand how they knew where everything was in the time of an emergency with little to no time to search for things. Carina ran the tip of her thumb across her lips, trying to come up with a better way to say what she felt. She could hear Tia cracking her knuckles and reached over, taking her hand and resting it on her lap. She didn't like seeing Tia anxious or overwhelmed, but she knew they needed to have this conversation.

Carina looked to her, frowning from how quickly Tia lowered her head. She didn't want to waste time figuring that out. "It's been a week. The kids are asking about you. What are you going to tell them?"

"What?" Tia didn't seem to register what she was asking.

"I'm not going to be the one to tell them you no longer want to see them."

Tia slumped back into the seat. She lifted her foot to the edge of the gurney, fear and anger merging in her chest. "Carina, I don't have time for this. I start my shift in 15 minutes."

"I'm sorry. You ignore all my calls and texts. If you want to end things because my sister freaked you out, or I did something to make you feel uncomfortable, fine. But I'm not going to keep doing this back and forth. We must stop this. If you want to end our friendship and stop seeing the kids…you brave up and tell them yourself." Every word rushed out with a mix of anxiety and sadness. Carina stepped out of the ambulance, leaving quickly so she wouldn't be seen crying.

Carina didn't know why she cared so much. A big part of her coming here was for her kids, but Carina couldn't deny that it was for herself too.

Chapter Ten

Tia

Tia had screwed up royally. She'd been doing that a lot, not sure of her place in Carina's life. And the confusion she felt was an outright punishment to the kids. After Carina's visit a few nights ago, Tia had spent most of her spare time analyzing her future.

For once, she needed to make a choice and stick with it. It was the only reason she hadn't contacted Carina since. She wasn't in high school. That time had long passed. Communication was the key to keeping any relationship alive.

"You okay there, partner?" Joe walked up, carrying two coffees in his hand. He handed her one and she leaned against the side of the ambulance. It was toward the end of their shift.

Tia had been trying to open up to the idea of having Joe as a partner. He was patient, much longer than she expected.

"Is it about that lady that came by a few nights ago?" Joe asked. Tia said nothing and he continued. "She your girlfriend or something?"

Tia looked at him, confused as to how he knew about her sexuality. It wasn't a secret, but she never said anything.

He smiled. "People gossip."

"Of course they do," she mumbled.

"So…"

Here was her shot to try. Tia sighed and took a sip of her coffee. "She's—she was my partner Bruce's wife." For some reason, Tia was scared to look up, ready to be judged. Not that Tia and Carina's friendship was wrong, but some people thought it was suspicious. Perhaps that's why Tia was hesitant in opening up further to Carina, feeling shame in their connection.

His brow perked up. It was obvious he wanted to know more.

"She's always been a friend. Not like now! Before, I only saw her through Bruce. There were no girl's nights out." Tia started to crack her knuckles, nervous about how much to share. "It's complicated."

Joe pursed his lips and shrugged. "Complicated," he repeated as if trying to determine its meaning. He drank some of his coffee and smiled. "Then uncomplicate it."

He walked around the ambulance and got inside. She stared dumbfounded by his response. She'd finally opened up and that's all he had to say. She stood there for some time, pondering how she could uncomplicate things.

Carina said she needed to live in the moment. All Tia could think about was Bruce and the loss his family endured every day. But that was the problem. She couldn't get past the sadness of not having him around, daydreaming about what he'd do on a specific call or how he'd be excited for Halloween. Bruce was gone. Saying his name in the present tense wouldn't change that. Carina and the kids couldn't afford to linger in the past.

No longer could she do the same.

*

"Thanks, for letting me come." Tia stood in the doorway while Carina stood emotionally guarded. She wore a thick black sweater that read *'Boo.'* It was Halloween and she knew they'd be going trick or treating soon. Carina's arms were folded.

After another week had passed since seeing Carina, Tia was stuck between contemplating what was right and second guessing herself. She'd called the kids telling them she'd be there tonight. "I told myself that you needed me to be strong. To help you keep Bruce's memories alive. Maybe that was wrong of me. Those kids of yours are a constant reminder of who we lost. Our memories keep him alive." Tia hoped Carina could feel her sincerity and smiled, wanting to prove to Carina she would do better.

Tia slid her hands in her front pockets. "I don't want to lose the kids because I genuinely love them." Tia stepped in closer, leaning her shoulder into the outer wall next to the door. She was a foot from Carina who seemed as nervous about this conversation as Tia was.

Carina played with the string on her sweater, too vulnerable to look Tia in the eyes. She cared so much for Tia, not sure if she'd hear from her again. Deep down, Carina knew Tia would come back for the kids. She just wasn't sure if Tia would come back for her too. Her heart beat fast when Tia closed the distance, inches away from each other.

"I miss you too." Tia's eyes were hopeful, exposing all her truths for Carina to see. The few weeks that past seemed like years. Tia missed the way Carina smiled when she walked into the house. She hoped it wasn't too late to get it all back with Carina and the kids.

It was all Carina needed to hear. Being mad at Tia felt wrong and pointless. She leaned in, Tia opening her arms to let her in as they embraced. It was like they could breathe again. Goosebumps ran up Tia's arms as a tear slipped from her eye. She was relieved. Time passed and the kids came into view.

Michelle approached first, dressed as a ninja. She wore the cutest smile. "You going trick or treating with us?" she asked, holding her pumpkin bucket.

Tia shrugged and looked to Carina for the answer.

"Yes, she is." Carina smiled. She opened the door wider, letting Tia in as Johnathan and Rina came into view in their costumes. "You three ready to go?" she asked.

They each said yes, and they were off.

After 45 minutes of trick or treating, Tia found herself trying to bribe the kids into having some of their candy. She even chased them down the block only ending up with nothing. An hour more passed when they made it around the last few blocks, back to the house.

Carina unlocked the doors, letting everyone in. Her kids dragged their feet inside, sleepy. "You three take off your shoes before you climb into bed," Carina called out as they headed to their rooms.

"This was great," Tia smiled, happy she had joined them. "I've never been trick or treating."

Her omission had Carina turn around swiftly in disbelief. "Never?" Taking a moment to process what Tia said, Carina walked into her living room and collapsed onto her couch. Tia did the same thing, falling beside her, both their legs stretched out.

"Well, yeah," she admitted. Tia shrugged and blew out slowly. "I just never had time to be that kind of kid."

"Your dad never tried to take you?" Carina asked.

Tia considered, twisting onto the couch to face Carina a few feet beside her. "Once." She frowned and shook her head. "I was maybe 10." Tia began visualizing her old memory. "He wanted to give me a real costume. I just wanted to go for the candy." Tia chuckled. Carina listened, fascinated by the story. "I waited at home. He said he'd be back in an hour. He was going to get me a costume. I was into *Mighty Morphin Power Rangers* at the time. The originals," Tia clarified, grinning.

"Of course," Carina chuckled. "Who didn't have a crush on Kimberly in her pink suit?"

Tia heard sarcasm and rolled her eyes. "Anyway, he was going to get me the green *Power Rangers costume*. I was a serious tomboy back then. I wanted to be Tommy."

"What happened?"

"Well…one hour turned into two and then two turned into the whole night." Tia shrugged. "He shoplifted the costume and was caught. Spent the night in jail." Tia ran her hand over her pants, distracting herself from that sad time in her life. "Not once have I ever hated my father. He made a lot of mistakes, but all to try and give me a better life. Did it work out in his favor? Most of the time, no."

"I've never met your father," Carina realized.

Tia nodded. "Bruce met him a few times."

"Invite him for dinner," Carina blurted out.

That took Tia a minute to process. "You want to meet him?" Tia asked, surprised.

"That's why I'm inviting him." She grinned.

That brought a smile to her face. "Well, he'll be away for about a month. He's a truck driver and he's taking an extended trip to make multiple deliveries so that he can be off for Christmas."

"Perfect. We can all have Christmas dinner together," Carina chimed.

"Don't you want to have it with your family? I mean, like your sisters and your parents."

"I will," Carina said. "But that'll be Christmas Eve. Christmas Day can be just for us."

That meant a lot for Tia to hear. "Okay. I'll let him know."

There was silence for a time. Carina broke it, getting out what was on her mind. "Tia…"

"Yeah."

"Don't make me chase you down again." Her tone was soft but firm. She made sure Tia saw what she was feeling and how serious she was about it.

Tia swallowed, hating that she'd hurt Carina and the kids whether they knew it or not. "I won't."

Carina smiled. "Good." Their eyes locked and the tension between them grew. Both of their hearts pounded. Breathing heavily, Carina dropped her eyes, closing them. She shifted her posture, averting her head to not feel so exposed. Carina couldn't tell what Tia was thinking and that made her nervous.

"I should—"

"Leave," Carina finished for Tia, aware of what she was about to say.

Tia nodded. "Yeah. But I really should go. Not for reasons you're thinking."

"Oh. What am I thinking?" Carina's voice came out in barely a whisper. That question seemed to hold a deeper meaning.

"I don't know." Tia faced forward, not able to look at Carina anymore. She closed her eyes, telling herself not to feel. Chills trailed all over her body as heat swam in her stomach.

"Drive home safe."

Tia smiled and stood. "I'll do that." Tia was both relieved and disappointed Carina didn't push to question what was on her mind.

They walked to the front door. "Please, let me know when you get there safe," Carina asked.

"I will. Night." Tia waved, walking to her car and feeling like she'd left her heart back inside the house.

Chapter Eleven

Carina

"Honey, we just don't understand why you want to spend Christmas Day at home." Carina's mom had been ranting about staying the night the moment they stepped through the door. The next few months rolled by fast and Carina could admit she was excited about Christmas. It was her favorite time of year, finding it much more special than most of her friends and family. Tia had spent an entire shift working on Thanksgiving and though Carina and the kids missed her, they ended up stopping by the station to drop off food to Tia after leaving her family's home.

After spending Thanksgiving with her entire family, Carina was looking forward to having a more intimate dinner with her kids, Tia, and Tia's father. It had been hard spending their first holidays without Bruce, but spending Christmas with her kids and Tia would be the medicine she needed. Carina and the kids needed to feel his physical absence. She'd cried so much in the last few weeks.

It was Christmas Eve and she promised to spend it with her parents like she did every year. Carina wanted to enjoy this evening and then take her kids home.

Her parents' home was large enough to fit everyone in the dining room. Sandra walked inside the house with her two boys and her husband Miguel and took off her coat. Her other sister Gina was on her way with her husband and 15 year-old daughter. It would be a full house.

Carina seated her kids at the table next to her as everyone began to take their seats. It was a formal dinner. Her parents took their seats a few minutes later. Her phone vibrated and Carina checked to see who it was. Tia had texted her *good luck.* Carina had been complaining all week about coming to this Christmas Eve dinner. She smiled, texted *thanks,* and put the phone away, finding her sister staring.

"Aunt Gina is here," Michelle cheered out.

Gina walked in with her daughter and husband, greeting the family. She went to their parents, giving them each a kiss before turning to Carina with a wide smile on her face.

"I'm hungry," Sandra's youngest boy whined.

"Quiet," Sandra chastised, taking her turn to hug her sister.

"All right. Let's get this evening started so my grandson doesn't starve." Carina's father chuckled.

They wasted no time serving dinner. The food was delicious. Carina always enjoyed her mom's cooking. She was distracted from all the food and mundane conversations until she heard Michelle telling them about tomorrow. Carina's mouth opened, planning to interrupt her daughter when she closed her mouth realizing it was too late. Carina hadn't gotten around to telling them what she'd be doing tomorrow.

Her family made no comments, but it was evident they were bothered by the news. When dinner was over, Carina's father excused all the kids from the table.

Carina leaned back into her chair, annoyed with how much her family seemed to question her every decision when it came to Tia being in her life. She slid the rest of her water glass further from within her reach, sweeping her brunette hair from her eyes.

"Should I even try and express how concerned we are about you?" Her father asked, as if speaking for the entire family. His eyes were narrowed on her as if ready to ground her for defiance.

Carina said nothing, biting at the inner wall of her cheek. She wanted to argue but Carina rolled her eyes, reminding herself she was no longer a child.

"What are you doing with your future? Next month will mark the year of Bruce's passing…"

Carina's eyes narrowed. "I don't need you to remind me of when my husband died," Carina spoke bitterly. She shut her eyes, taking a breath. "My relationship with Tia is my own and has nothing to do with Bruce."

"So, you admit, you have a relationship with this woman?" Sandra asked.

"I think we should trust Carina and what's best for her," her eldest sister Gina stated in Carina's defense.

Carina looked to her sister Gina and smiled with tears in her eyes.

"I don't think you understand, Gina. Tia…she's—"

"Gay. A lesbian," Carina finished for her sister Sandra. "I figured I'd help you since you were struggling so terribly." She rolled her eyes. "I don't know what the issue is, but I do know I won't end my friendship with Tia to please any of you. I'm making this very clear to you all right now. You bad mouth Tia to my kids once and from now on you'll be talking to them over the phone, supervised." Carina stood fast, shoving the chair back with the back of her legs, and called her kids downstairs.

"You don't have to leave," her mother pleaded.

"Actually, I do!"

*

The thought of having to distance herself from her family was terrifying. They could be too protective even when they didn't need to be. The only way to make them back off was to give them an ultimatum. Spending the rest of Christmas Eve at home, they'd played board games. Now that it was Sunday, Carina was thankful she'd have the day with Tia and the kids. No distractions.

Carina had been cooking all day, going beyond her cooking limits to make today perfect. She was expecting Tia and her father at any minute. "Hey Johnathan, I need you to turn your game off."

"Mom, just five more minutes," he whined.

"No! Off now," she shouted from the kitchen.

"When's Tia coming?" Michelle asked for the seventh time.

Her kids were excited to spend Christmas with Tia while Carina was nervous. Her belly had been flipping all day. "Soon honey." Carina looked in the crock pot, checking on the roast. It was nearly done. She'd baked mac and cheese and ham in the oven. Bruce had told her once how much Tia loved ham and mac and cheese. She also had cornbread stuffing since that was Tia's favorite and green bean casserole. She might've gone overboard but Carina didn't care. She wanted everything to be perfect.

"Relax. It's just Tia. And her dad." She smiled, talking to herself.

"Why are you so nervous, Mom?" Rina asked.

"I'm not," Carina responded in a squeaking voice. "Okay, I am. I just want Tia's father to feel welcomed."

"He will, Mom," Rina assured her. The doorbell rang and Carina froze. "I'll get it," Rina shouted and ran to the front door.

Carina washed her hands and dried them, hearing Tia from the front of the house. She walked into the living room, finding Johnathan still playing his video game. She walked up, shaking her head and turning off the TV.

"Mom," he hissed.

"I swear, Johnathan, I'll donate your Xbox to Goodwill. I better not see you touch it again today." She gave him a look that held much promise.

Tia walked in, giving Johnathan a look that said she heard everything. Johnathan smiled shyly, standing up to greet the man standing beside her. Tia reached out, putting her hand over his head and messing up his hair. "Don't give your mom a hard time," she whispered in his ear.

Johnathan smiled awkwardly and nodded.

"Hello. You must be Johnathan." Tia's father held his hand out.

"Yes sir." Johnathan shook the man's hand and smiled. "Can we eat now, Mom?"

Carina shook her head. "Johnathan, go wash your hands." Carina smiled. "Sorry about that." She held out her hand. "I'm Carina."

"Oh, I know! My daughter talks about you and your lovely kids a lot."

Carina watched Tia blush. "Oh, does she?" Carina encouraged him to continue.

"Dad." Tia shook her head, giving her father a long look.

"Fine. I won't embarrass you just yet." He patted her shoulder. "How can I help?"

"You don't have to," Carina said. "You're our guest."

"Trust me. Let him help." Tia smiled.

The food was about done, and all that was left was to set up the table. She worked beside Tia's father setting the table and placing the food at the center. Soon everyone gathered around the table and Carina knew this dinner would be better than last night's. The kids wasted no time in stuffing their mouths. Johnathan had overeaten, gaining a stomach ache.

"I'll go help them settle in for the night," Tia offered.

Alone, Carina smiled to Tia's father, nervous to speak to him. He'd raised Tia alone. There was still a lot she didn't know about Tia's life. Like what happened to her mother. She didn't want to be invasive and figured when the time was right, she'd ask Tia herself.

"I appreciate you opening your home up to me. I don't think I've had a cooked meal like that in years." She could tell he was being sincere.

"You're welcome here at any time. And I'll make sure whenever Tia comes over, I send her back home with leftovers."

"Yeah. Since she moved out, I'll have to go knocking on her door to get that, but I appreciate it." He smiled and took another bite from his plate.

Carina hadn't known Tia moved out. Tia had a habit of leaving out important details about her own life. She would table what she learned for later. "I'll make sure I pack leftovers before you leave."

"You're very kind." He smiled and placed his fork on the plate. "You care for my daughter?" he asked.

Carina smiled. "Yes. I do!"

He smiled but it didn't reach his eyes. "I'm not going to always be here for her. I need to know…you'll always be someone she can lean on."

"I'm not going anywhere." Carina sighed and looked down at her plate. Tia's father was all she truly had.

Tia came back downstairs, wearing a Santa hat.

"Where'd you get that?" Carina chuckled.

It didn't quite fit her head with Tia's dreads being in the way. It was covered in sparkles with Tia's name written at the center. "Michelle made it for me at school. It's my Christmas present."

"Lucky," Carina grinned.

"It's not luck. She said I'm her favorite."

"I'm her mom. I will always be her favorite."

Tia chuckled and stuck her tongue out. "Don't be jealous." She took a seat and Carina tried to reach across the table to take it. Tia pivoted back and snorted. "Jealousy looks cute on you."

Tia noticed her father watching the both of them, a small smile forming on his face.

"Yes, it does," Carina agreed confidently.

They joked for some time until Tia's father announced he had to leave. They'd driven in separate vehicles which made Carina happy. She wasn't ready to see Tia leave yet. Carina provided Tia's father two containers full of leftovers, saying goodbye to him at the door.

Tia lingered next to the door, watching her father pull away.

"What are the kids doing?" Carina asked, standing beside her, watching Tia.

"Well, Michelle passed out on me. Rina is listening to music and texting her friends probably. And Johnathan knows he's on a gaming restriction, so he's probably lying in bed acting miserable."

"All sounds accurate," Carina joked.

She waited for Tia to move out of the doorway to close it, noticing the mistletoe above them. Her kids thought it would be cute to have it up. Carina tried to act like she didn't notice but it was too late.

Tia followed her sight, staring up at the mistletoe too.

Carina's skin flushed as it took Tia a long time to make eye contact. When Tia did face her again, her eyes had zoned in on her lips. Suddenly, she felt self-conscious, wanting to do something to distract them.

"We always put it up every year. Bruce said it was his way of finding a cheap excuse to kiss me," Carina explained. Mentioning Bruce's name ended whatever tension had grown between them. Memories of Bruce came swarming into her mind, him pulling her into kisses or calling her to the door just to kiss her under the mistletoe. Sometimes, he'd keep the mistletoe up past New Year's just to be funny.

Carina found herself walking into the living room, standing next to the Christmas tree. Tia followed her, standing a safe emotional distance away. She'd seen the sadness surface in Carina's eyes, knowing the holidays were hard to celebrate. Carina needed to put on a brave face for her kids.

"You don't have to pretend with me," Tia said. She walked up. "He'll always be the man who told goofy Christmas stories or made ridiculous New Year's resolutions."

"Yeah," Carina beamed. She reached down for a small box and held it up, locking eyes with Tia and waiting for her to grab it.

"What's this?"

"You have to open it," Carina said.

Tia narrowed her eyes and took the box. She opened the small, palm sized box, finding a set of keys inside. Tia frowned. "I don't understand."

"Bruce told me how he'd show off his motorcycle to you and you'd threaten to steal it one day. I could never drive that thing. I know he'd want you to have it."

"I, I can't," Tia shook her head.

"You can and you will." Carina's tone made that final.

She stared, astounded by the gift and headed toward the garage door connected through the kitchen. She went inside, turning on the light and removed the tarp over the motorcycle. Tia's smile was huge as she ran her fingers over its slick design. Carina stood in the doorway, grinning from ear to ear, watching as Tia admired her new gift.

It meant a lot to see Tia so happy. Bruce had been right in Tia loving his motorcycle more than him. Tia squealed, running up to Carina. She pulled her into a hug, squeezing her tightly.

Carina melted into Tia's form and squeezed back, taking a breath, the aroma from Tia's body wash perfuming her nose. Tia smelled of something flowery. Carina twirled her index finger around one of Tia's dreads, running her thumb over it. Something new blossomed inside Carina and she took a minute to process it. She loved touching Tia. Running her fingers over Tia's dreads.

Their embrace loosened, Tia creating enough distance to look into Carina's eyes. There was so much tension between them a knife could make a clean slice straight through. Tia's eyes darkened. "Thank you," she whispered, almost breathless.

Carina swallowed her tongue, unable to form a response. In the past year their relationship had gone from casual friendship to something much deeper and meaningful. Carina's arms were still wrapped around Tia's neck. She could hear her heart beating fast in her ears. There was this magnetic pull to close the distance between them. She closed her eyes, pressing her forehead into Tia's nose. She took in a long breath. Tia had been Bruce's best friend and partner. The thought of Bruce made her pull away.

Whatever she was feeling or about to do, she really needed to consider the outcome. "I'm glad you like your gift," she whispered. She couldn't look at Tia just yet.

Tia cleared her throat. "I do. I got you one too." Tia knew that whatever was happening between them she could no longer hide from it. She pulled out a long thin box from her back pocket and held it out, taking a step back.

Carina looked up and reached for it slowly. They were still in the garage, the cold outside air making her skin form chills. She turned to head into the house, opening up the box. She wasn't ready to face Tia yet. She looked inside, finding a gold chained necklace with a pendant attached.

"You can open it up," Tia explained.

She did, her back turned to Tia the entire time. Inside was a small picture of her and Bruce on one side and their kids on the other. Carina shut her eyes, a tear slipping out.

"It was hard finding a place that could take one of your photos and make it that small. I just thought...I don't know. I look up to you guys and what a family should look like."

Carina found the courage to turn and face Tia and smiled. "Tia…this is…" She felt more tears slip from her eyes and wiped them away. "As long as there is love, a family could look like many things. It means a lot to know that you see that kind of love in us."

"Of course." Tia smiled. "I promise I'll take good care of it," she said, looking at the key in her hand. "I should get going. Working a double tomorrow."

Carina smiled. "K!" She walked Tia to the front door and couldn't find the courage to give her a hug. They said their goodnights and Carina watched her go.

*

"How's my little sis doing?" Gina came up to the table at the Mexican restaurant they frequented, giving her a kiss on the cheek.

Carina had been nervous the last few weeks. After Christmas, Tia came around every week but there had been awkwardness when they were alone. New Year's passed and in a few weeks, it'd be one year since losing Bruce.

There was no way of knowing her life would change this much in one year. The memory of his death had increased for her and her kids. Even more, her conflicting feelings regarding Tia had made it hard for her to get through the day. It was no surprise to her that she could be attracted to a woman. Carina had been on a few dates with women before Bruce, but she never had time to define for herself what it meant to be attracted to women and men. Now at 35 it no longer mattered to her if she should define herself. She felt what she felt and that was enough for her.

But Tia wasn't just any woman. She'd played a big role in Bruce's life. Carina never wanted to cross a line that could offend her husband's bond with Tia. She didn't know if it was wrong being attracted to Tia because that's what she felt. She was very attracted to Tia, but it didn't mean she was ready for a new relationship. Carina knew she needed more time. But these feelings were present, and she couldn't ignore them anymore.

She needed to talk to someone open minded and willing to listen. Carina smiled nervously. "I'm…surviving," Carina finally responded.

Gina nodded and looked up. "I asked Sandra to come too."

Carina gave her sister a death stare, shaking her head into her hand. Perhaps she was wrong in trusting Gina to have this private conversation. Carina had a few close friends she could've gone too, but she was much closer to her sisters. Usually, she and Sandra never had disagreements, until now.

"You have to give her a chance to listen. I'll be right here. I'm on your side." Gina smiled and Carina caved in. She didn't really have a choice.

Sandra approached, giving Gina a hug and then turned to Carina, cautious of how she'd react. She held up both hands. "I come in piece."

Carina waved for her to sit. "I surely hope so."

They ordered their food and Carina stalled, making an excuse for Tia. She was picking the kids up from their afterschool programs. Both her sisters waited until she put her phone away.

"You wanted to talk," Sandra said.

Carina nodded and looked to her sister Sandra. The fact that she didn't support her friendship with Tia and had suspicions only made her more uncomfortable to speak her truth.

"Look, Carina. Whatever you have to say, I'll listen. I only want the best for you." Gina smiled. "I love you."

"I never thought I'd survive the first year without Bruce." Carina only had her truth and hoped she wouldn't be judged for it. "I never had a plan B. He was it." Carina tried not to cry but it was hard with it being so close to the anniversary of his passing. "No matter what your reasons are for being so against Tia, I took what mattered most from your words. I know I can do this with or without anyone's help now! I'm a single parent. I finally accept that and have the ability to be one."

Her sisters did their part in listening.

It'd been years since Carina was in this position. It was like starting over again. The attraction she felt for Tia was real and she didn't know what to do with it. She'd barely been an adult when she met Bruce. It was easy with him. With Tia, there was so much ahead of them if Carina even considered her a possibility.

Gina reached out seeing how hard it was for Carina to open up to them. "You have feelings for someone new?" she asked, already knowing who it was.

There was hesitation. Carina acknowledged her sister and smiled sheepishly. She snuck a peak to Sandra whose expression was unreadable. "I'm attracted to Tia. I always knew there was something tender between us…but I wasn't ready to acknowledge it."

"And you're ready now?" Sandra asked, her tone a bit harsh. She let out a sharp exhale.

"Yes!" She narrowed her eyes at Sandra. "I want to make something clear. Tia is not the first woman I've felt something for. Before Bruce, there were two separate occasions I went out with a woman."

Sandra's eyes widened and she looked to her other sister, searching for shock.

"I remember one night you left with some friends to go to the movies." Gina gave Carina a knowing smile. "I knew you were lying. When you tried to explain what the movie was about you got that movie mixed up with another. I thought you were sneaking off to see a boy. I watched your friends go into the movie theater and you run across the parking lot to a girl and kiss her. Then you took off in her car."

"You never said anything," Sandra said, shocked.

"It wasn't my secret to tell." Gina shrugged. "A few years later you met Bruce and it no longer mattered. I knew you loved him."

Carina smiled, never knowing her sister had followed her that night. "In telling you this…your whole theory of Tia influencing me is wrong!" Carina said to Sandra and continued. "I'm very aware of who she is. Every time I try to forget, I think of Bruce and feel guilty. I don't know if he'd approve. His sarcastic side would tell me never to fall in love again. But his serious side… I don't know."

"You're in love with her?" Sandra asked wry in her question.

"That's not what she's saying, Sandra." Gina seemed to do the chastising. "I get that we were brought up to believe in certain things. But we can't control what we feel, and everyone is entitled to love who they love."

"I know," Sandra grimaced. "I just see people out there who are threatened and looked at differently for being gay. I don't want that for you! It's not that I hate Tia or the idea of you with her. I'm just scared for how people will treat you and your kids."

"All I care about is how you and our conservative parents will treat me and my kids." Carina smiled, pinching the bridge of her nose. "I'm not ready to find some new romance. Bruce is still all I think about. I can't picture someone else being the front runner to my heart. Not yet. I just know I feel..." Carina couldn't manage to say the words without her skin warming with a heat she thought she'd never feel again.

"You really see something with this woman?" Sandra smiled weakly. "Tia," she said, trying to be respectful and finally acknowledge Tia for who she is. Someone of value and importance.

"I know it's barely been a year. I shouldn't be thinking about her at all. Especially her."

"You can always ignore how you feel," Gina said, taking a sip of her water.

"I can't," Carina said adamantly.

Sandra grinned. "You walked into that one."

Carina looked to Gina and rolled her eyes. Gina was known for her reverse psychology and Carina wasted no time falling into that emotional trap. "I don't know what to do," Carina said, sounding defeated.

"You don't have to do anything. At least not today. But maybe tomorrow, or after you visit your husband's grave you can at least talk to Tia and see how she feels. You don't have to act on it. Just acknowledge it." Gina gave great advice.

In a sigh of relief, Carina thanked both of her sisters for listening and not giving her a hard time. When it mattered, they would always give her the support she needed.

Chapter Twelve

Tia

Tia sat in the ambulance drumming her fingers against the steering wheel. They'd been put on standby for the past 20 minutes for a house fire. Sitting two blocks from the actual fire in a neighborhood that was known for drug pushing, Tia made sure they kept all their doors locked and windows rolled up.

"You've been quiet." Joe started to eat some crackers. His foot rested atop the dashboard. He held out his crackers, offering Tia some.

"I have a lot on my mind."

Joe grunted. "Like…"

Tia shrugged, turning up the sound to her walkie talkie attached to her pants belt. "Today is—Bruce died a year ago today."

There was silence. He put his crackers in his bag and set it between their chairs. "You should've taken the day off."

"Why? So I can stay at home and get lost in my head?"

"No! I don't know what you could do, but not that. That option sounds depressing."

Tia snorted.

"Don't you want to spend it with Carina and those awesome kids you talk about?"

Tia frowned, paying attention to what he was saying. "I already know he's gone."

"Do you?"

Tia glanced at Joe, pursing her lips in frustration. "What the hell are you talking about?"

"The few times she's come by, it's clear there's this energy between you two. And every time you've mentioned Bruce and how he was with his family…it's like you still see him alive, physically present. It's stopping you from stepping forward to the possibilities. You're not stealing his family."

"There's nothing going on between…"

Joe twisted in his seat to face Tia head on, not being deluded by her statement. "You want to try that lie again?"

Tia said nothing else, knowing she'd only sound defensive.

"This is dispatch to Medic 111. You're clear to go on scene."

Tia straightened, clearing her mind of personal issues and put the ambulance into drive. It took them less than a minute to pull up on scene, parking behind the roll of fire trucks. The house was badly burned, smoke still exiting. They hopped out, being guided by fire fighters in full gear up to the porch where their patient lay unconscious.

"We barely found him. He hid underneath the bed. I guess he thought he wouldn't get burned." The fire fighter pulled off his helmet, helping them place him on the gurney right away.

"I'm going to need my partner in the back. Is the fire out?" Joe asked.

"Yeah!" The firefighter shouted. "Captain, can we spare one to go with them?" His captain gave him a thumbs up and he nodded.

It took them a minute to load the patient in the back of the ambulance. Tia grabbed her shears, working right away to cut off all the patients clothing. She noticed his hair and nose hair was singed. His face was spared of second or third degree burns.

Tia placed a mask over their patient's face, turning it up to 15 liters of oxygen.

"I need to intubate him, now!" Joe shouted. "Let's go," he yelled to the fire fighter to start driving to the hospital. There was no time to waste in a situation this critical.

The right side of his body was burned the most. His skin was red with thick blisters. All his hair was singed on the right side. The patient had second and third degree burns over his chest down to his lower left leg, his skin darkened all over.

"Damn it." Joe sneered.

Tia reached in the cabinet and pulled out a small mac intubation blade that would help give a curvier glide for the tube. She checked the patient's temperature. It was dropping, his body no longer capable of maintaining heat.

"Got it," he called out.

Moving with precision, Tia upped the oxygen, forcing air down their patient's lungs, squeezing the bag valve every couple of seconds. Joe moved to start an I.V. in their patient's left arm.

Joe grabbed a couple of warm blankets underneath the bench and covered up the patient. Tia sat in the captain's chair behind the patient's head, reaching the hospital on the intercom. Tia spoke clearly and calmly.

"This is Medic 111. Bringing you a 33 year-old male. Patient was in a house fire, found unconscious with partial and full thickness burns over 36 percent of his body…" As she gave the report, the patient's saturation began to drop. He was headed into cardiac arrest. She gave them an update and ended her call.

They pulled up to the emergency department, a few nurses already standing outside to assist them. Tia continued to force air into her patient's lungs as they reached their designated room. Respiratory therapy was present and took over, Tia taking a step around to help slide the patient over to the hospital bed and off the gurney.

It took them over 30 minutes to clear from the hospital, the back of the ambulance looking like a tornado tore everything apart. Anytime they had a critical patient, the ambulance could get messy fast.

"Fuck," Joe hissed, going over his charting. "This sucks. I could've had a chest tube in him fast." As a combat medic he could have, but as a paramedic in this location it was outside of his scope of practice.

All that energy and she had nowhere to put it. Tia wanted to do more but she had her limits too. For the first time, she wished she was a paramedic. *Damn*. Who would've thought Bruce's words would haunt her.

*

The next evening, Tia had her day off. She'd slept when the sun went down. Before she knew it, she was at Carina's front porch, holding out a container of ice cream and a bottle of wine.

The kids were in bed when Tia sat on the floor near the fireplace. She held her glass of wine, staring at the flames as they ate away at the log inside. She had so much on her mind, needing to get out some of her thoughts. Carina sat beside her, leaning her back into the couch. Her posture was still as if she was on the verge of cracking. "I thought you'd take the night off. The kids and I were hoping you'd join us in visiting Bruce at the cemetery."

Joe had been right. Tia should've taken the day off with Carina and the kids. Tia faced Carina's guarded eyes and pictured Bruce sitting right behind her.

The music in the background filled the silence between them. Tia knew avoiding Carina's feelings would be a mistake. "I thought…it was best for you and your family to visit him on your own."

"You are a part of our family, Tia." Carina's eye held sincerity but also frustration.

Tia sighed. "You know what I mean."

"Actually, I don't!" Carina looked up at the ceiling trying not to get upset. She blinked away tears before facing her again. "While you chose to work, I was split between making sure my kids were okay and making sure you were."

"I'm okay," Tia lied. Now, Tia finally understood what Bruce was talking about every time he upset Carina. Tia never wanted to upset her again.

"But I didn't know that, Tia! And right now, you don't look okay." Carina spoke calmly though her frustration was building. She wondered why Tia couldn't open up enough to express her true feelings.

Unsure of how to respond, Tia waited for Carina to relax enough to hear her out. "If I'd known it meant this much to you for me to take the night off, I'd have done it."

"I'm sorry. Maybe you're right." Carina stood, not paying attention and spilling her wine that sat between her thighs. "Fuck!" she hissed, dropping down to her knees to wipe off the carpet before it stained. She looked around for anything to clean up the spill and stood again, moving into the kitchen.

Tia took a few breaths and followed her into the kitchen. Tia could hear Carina crying the moment she stepped inside. It broke Tia's heart to hear Carina in so much pain. She placed her glass on the counter and ambled slowly toward her. Tia reached out, grazing her fingers over Carina's shoulder. Gradually, Tia pulled Carina into her body, embracing her from behind. Tia's arm curled around Carina's waist, and she rested her cheek against the back of her head. Tia knew the moment she began holding Carina she didn't want to let go. This wasn't how friends hugged. It was intimate and breathtakingly arousing. Tia swallowed the lump in her throat. "I'm sorry. I'm doing everything wrong," she whispered softly.

"It's not you! I'm putting too much on you because of how I'm feeling," Carina admitted.

There was silence. Tia knew it would take time for Carina to regain her composure. She took advantage of the silence and chose to speak. "My partner tells me I keep living in the past as if Bruce could walk in here any moment. It annoys the shit out of me that he's right."

"What are you afraid of?" Carina asked softly.

Tia had been drifting into the sound of Carina's breathing. Carina felt right in her arms. Everything about this felt right but also wrong. She shouldn't want this feeling. Out of all the women Tia came across, Carina should've never been who she wanted. It wasn't right. How could she say all that to Carina? She wasn't naïve. She'd been noticing the way Carina looked at her too.

Soft delicate hands grazed over the arm she had curled around Carina's waist. Tia stifled a moan when Carina pressed into her, their bodies fully aligned. Tia's arm tightened around her, not wanting to let her go. It was hard being like this. At any moment, Tia would need to move away or kiss Carina. Just the thought burned a path down to her core.

"Tia..." Carina whispered through a heavy breath. Chills ran up Tia's arms from the way Carina said her name. She twisted to face Tia, staring into her eyes and slowly drifting down to her lips. Carina licked her own, leaning in closer.

The thought of kissing Carina caused wetness to fill between Tia's legs for the first time. Before she lost restraint, Tia closed her eyes. "We can't," she whimpered, hating her own words.

"You think this is easy for me?" Carina asked, frustrated and ready to breakdown. "I feel like I just lost him yesterday. You were his best friend. I never thought I'd feel again." Carina shook her head and hid her face in the crook of Tia's neck. "I ask myself, why you? Out of anyone."

"So why me?" Tia whispered, needing to know.

Carina looked back into Tia's eyes. "At first, it was because you understood who I lost. But now, it's because you make me feel like anything's possible. That I'm strong and beautiful. Because you have such a big heart and you do things without expectation. You love my kids. You make me happy even when I think I should be feeling sad. Tia...it's simply because it's just you."

"I don't know—I don't want to insult or—"

"Tia. Bruce is gone!" Carina forced the words out for herself and for Tia.

That one statement was louder than everything else they'd said to each other in the past year.

"I don't know what this is. But I no longer want to hide from it. I'm asking you not to hide from it. I'm a grown woman. I know what I need. I have no idea what I'm doing, but I know how I feel." Carina was determined to finally own all her feelings. She wouldn't feel ashamed.

"I suppose you do."

Carina relaxed, thankful Tia was no longer questioning how she felt and brushed the tips of her fingers down Tia's jaw. She watched as Tia closed her eyes, pressing lightly into her touch. "I need to hear you say it. That I'm not the only one feeling this."

What little air remained in Tia's lungs seemed to not matter as she became lightheaded. There was fear in telling the truth. If Tia admitted to anything, it would make everything real. She opened her eyes again, Carina watchful. "Can you really look past everything?"

"Tia, I'm not going to pretend and say Bruce's memories aren't standing in between us. They are. But that's all they are. Memories. And when I think about the kind of man he was, he'd want me to try and move on. He'd want you to move on too."

"But you?"

Carina shrugged. "I'm sure he never pictured himself dying and who he'd pick to replace him. I know he'd support any decision I made as long as I ended up happy." Carina cupped Tia's chin with the palm of her hand. "I need to hear it."

"You know I care about you." Tia took a breath, finding the courage in saying what needed to be said. "You're so strong. I think about you all the time. Yes, I like you so much it scares me."

Carina sighed in relief, burying her face into Tia's neck. "Thank you! I felt like I was pulling your teeth to get you to admit that."

Tia laughed. "Sorry I'm making it hard for you. You know, I've never done this, so…"

"Done what?" Carina looked up. She took a step back, losing contact from Tia's body. She felt an absence, wanting to go back to her but not wanting to be too clingy. A ridiculous feeling.

"This." Tia waved her hand back and forth between them. "Felt so swept away by emotions. Wanted someone so much that it scares me." She'd shared more than she intended. Tia shifted, nervous. "I mean, I've been in relationships. I even came close to falling in love once. But it was over before I could even feel…what I'm feeling now, for you."

"You didn't have to tell me that, but I'm glad you did."

Able to take a breath without feeling so scared, Tia waved out her arms. "Now what?"

Carina shook her head. "I don't know! I guess…I still…"

"I know. Me too. I don't want to start anything with the anxiety of Bruce standing over my shoulder. That wouldn't be fair to either of us. Especially the kids."

"Agreed." Carina smiled. "I'll need to tell them about us."

Tia nodded, nervous all over again.

She cracked a knuckle and Carina reached out, linking both their hands together in reassurance.

"Hey! They love you," Carina reminded Tia, squeezing her hands firmly.

"I know."

"Let's just continue being us. We were friends first. There's so much I want to know about you. We'll know when we're ready."

"Deal."

Chapter Thirteen

Carina

"Will you be my valentine, Mommy?" Michelle held a card with a flower in the middle and surrounded by hearts that she drew in class. Coming home, that was the first thing she pulled out of her backpack.

"You can't be Mommy's valentine," Johnathan intruded.

Michelle's expression skewed in confusion. "Why not?"

"Because Tia's her valentine," Johnathan explained.

A blush crept up over Carina's cheeks. "I can have two valentines."

"Tia won't mind," Michelle argued, sticking her tongue out at her brother.

"Anything for the upcoming birthday girl," Carina cheered, pulling her daughter into her arms.

Michelle giggled as Carina pulled her in for hugs and kisses. "Mommy, I'm too big for that."

"Never." Carina gave her daughter a big kiss on the cheek. She looked up to Johnathan as he took a step back. "None of you are."

Carina stood, giving a mischievous grin.

Her son took off as she chased after him. He screamed, telling Rina to run as they were all chased around the house for kisses.

Carina ended up lying on the living room floor, exhausted from chasing her kids. She twisted her head, hearing footsteps come her way.

Rina approached. "Mom, can I talk to you?"

"Of course." Carina scooted up, leaning back into the couch. Her daughter sat beside her. "What's on your mind?"

She sighed and looked away. Whatever was on her mind, she'd been struggling with it emotionally for some time.

Carina knew something was bothering her daughter but knew she needed to be patient. When a tear slid down her daughter's cheek, Carina reached over, wiping it with her thumb. "You can tell me anything and I'd never be mad at you for it."

Rina sighed with a nod. "Remember when we walked in on you and Tia sleeping?"

Carina nodded.

Her daughter lowered her head. "I pretended it didn't hurt. I told Aunt Sandra, even before that morning, that Daddy wouldn't like you being so close to Tia."

That made Carina silent. She'd been adamant in believing her kids weren't bothered by how close Tia and she had gotten, declaring Sandra was overreacting, but her daughter had gone to her aunt in confidence. Sandra had been a good aunt in not telling her what Rina said, whereas otherwise she was usually the judgmental sister.

"I'm sorry, Mom. I know you and Aunt Sandra were mad at each other and it was because of me. I felt bad for saying it, but I was still so angry and scared you were trying to forget Dad."

Carina shook her head, pulling her daughter in for a hug. "You have nothing to feel guilty about. I wish your father was still here too, honey. I will never forget or try to replace him or his memories. Never."

Rina pulled back and held her mother's eyes with strength. "I know now—he isn't coming back. He was the best Dad."

"He was the best husband," Carina said and smiled.

"And a best friend," Rina smiled back. "He only had two best friends Mom. You and Tia."

Carina nodded.

"He wouldn't want you to be alone. So, if you're not with Tia because of us, I already talked to Michelle and Johnathan and we agreed; it would be okay."

Carina shuddered, tears falling from her eyes. Hearing her daughter say those words meant a lot to her. Her kids were so open minded and understanding.

"I even told Aunt Sandra that I was no longer worried and hope you and Tia work out."

"You did?" Carina asked astonished. When had her daughter grown up? She stared at Rina in amazement and pulled her in, giving her a big kiss on the cheek.

"Mom," Rina whined but didn't pull away.

"I love you."

*

The kids screamed as Uncle Miguel chased them around in a villain costume. Luckily, it wasn't raining today in late February weather. The clouds were out but not dark and threatening.

Everyone was gathered in the backyard of Carina's home for the celebration.

Michelle was turning eight. Carina wanted to give her daughter a special birthday party since last year they didn't do anything with Bruce passing only a month prior. Hotdog, chips, and pizza were served as the kids ate away and played.

Sandra walked up, bumping shoulders with Carina as they watched their kids playing together. "They grow up so fast."

"Yes, they do!" Carina agreed, sighing as she wished she could keep Michelle young for as long as possible.

Sneaking a peak toward her sister, Carina remembered when they were kids and nothing could get in between them. Sandra always had her back and she didn't want to ever forget that. Carina hadn't seen her sister much and wanted to talk to her about what Rina shared a week ago. The kids ran past them near the entrance leading into the house and Sandra bumped against Carina to avoid them. When Sandra looked at her, Carina smiled taking this chance to speak. "Look, Sandra. I talked to Rina and she told me what she told you months ago." She'd been so angry at her sister, thinking she was as homophobic as their parents. "I'm sorry. I thought…"

"Don't worry about it! You were still too deep in grief to see and I could've come to you about it in a different way. Truth is I was acting prejudiced. Not because I think Tia is some bad influence, but I was afraid. There are so many people who want to see the LGBT community fall apart, who see them as weak. I was scared for you and that scared me. I'm sorry." Sandra smiled, reaching out to squeeze Carina's forearm.

Carina nodded, relieved to hear those words.

"What matters now is that your kids are happy. With all of it. And you're happy." A few heartbeats passed as

Sandra studied her sister. "*Are* you happy?" Sandra asked, attentive to her response.

Carina looked around in the crowd, finding Tia playing with the kids. She watched for awhile, in need of some alone time with Tia. In the last month, they talked everyday about anything that was on their minds. What they needed now was time for just the two of them. Tia sensed Carina staring and smiled, causing Carina's breath to grow heavy. "We're taking things slow."

"How slow?" Sandra reached out and squeezed her sister's hand. "There's no time table when it comes to feelings. There's no magical button that tells you when you're allowed to move on. If you're ready, go for it. And if you're hoping our parents will fall in love with the idea of you two, let that dream die. Do what's best for you two! You know you have my support and Gina's. I really mean that. I'm sorry if I made you doubt that I never did. I was honestly just afraid you'd skip healing and fall into a loveless relationship to dull your pain."

Carina looked at her sister and smiled. "I'm thankful we haven't moved too quickly." Carina chuckled, thinking of the many times in the past few weeks she wanted to skip a few steps and climb right into bed with Tia. "And it means a lot to know I have your support too!"

"Go on." Sandra nodded toward Tia and walked away, leaving Carina with much to think about.

*

Toward the end of the party, everyone gathered to sing happy birthday to Michelle as she stood near her birthday cake her grandma baked. Michelle tried blowing out the candles. Two were left and she looked over to Tia, waving for her to help.

Michelle grabbed Tia's hand as they blew together, the flame of the candles dissipating. They cheered as everyone clapped.

Cake was served, all the kids sitting at the table eating and chatting together. Carina smiled and walked over to the far end of the backyard, trying not to hover in front of her daughter's friends. Tia walked over, offering Carina a slice of cake and sat in a chair right beside her.

"Thanks!" Carina took a bite, moaning from the delightful taste. She peeked toward Tia, realizing she was without some cake and squinted her eyes playfully. "Don't tell me you don't like cake all of a sudden."

Tia grinned. "I do! I'm several pounds over my weight and I'd like to stop there before it turns into a lingering 20."

Stunned, Carina tilted her head back, giving Tia's body a full intake. "From what I can see you look very good and fit. Those arms." She wiggled her brows.

"I think you're a little biased."

Carina shrugged. "A little. But I would never lie to you. You are…" She looked into Tia's eyes and then down to her mouth.

Someone approached, clearing their throat. Carina smiled, acknowledging her father.

Tia stood, but Carina reached over and squeezed her thigh. Carina stared at her father, confident in herself and what she felt. "Did you need something, Papa?"

His eyes scanned his daughter, trying to find some weakness that could get her to submit to his views. Carina only stared back with stubborn eyes, straightening her posture. "Carina! I need to talk to you privately," he said in rushed tone, too rigid and angry to hide his emotions.

"Today is about Michelle. Anything you have to say—if it isn't urgent—can wait till tomorrow." Carina held onto Tia until she sat back down.

"Your mother cannot take you doing this to her. It is obvious you're openly flirting with this woman. In front of everyone. Some of us can hear you!" His tone was low but sharp. "What kind of mother would do such a thing in front of her children?"

"The kind that has the ability to teach her kids that there is more than one way to love," Tia said firmly. She wasn't planning to speak but his disrespect in talking to Carina as if she was a bad mother pissed her off.

Carina locked eyes with Tia and smiled, grateful to have her here. "Papa, I love you and Mom. I hope that one day you can really respect what I intend to have with Tia. And what she has with my kids."

He scowled and shook his head, waving his hand out and walking off. It didn't take him long to reach his wife and pack to leave. Carina shook her head disappointed in her parents. She found her kids saying bye to their grandparents and let them have their moment.

"You really want to see this through between us?" Tia asked quietly.

Carina relaxed her shoulders, no longer scared of the future. "I know what I want. My kids stand behind us. My sisters do too. I have to believe that Bruce would be happy for us. I can't let fear dictate me. This isn't some small crush." Carina reached for Tia's hand, pulling it into her lap. "When you're ready, I'll be waiting." She leaned in, the nearness of Tia making her breathless, and kissed her cheek. "I should go and check on the kids."

Tia smiled and nodded. "I'm not going anywhere."

*

The party ended an hour later. Being a supportive sister, Gina offered to take the kids for the night. Her way of giving Carina no excuse to let Tia leave without them having private time.

Carina's thoughts no longer sought out passionate romance for Bruce. She'd never forget their time spent together, but her heart knew long before her mind that he could no longer give her what she needed. In the last month, she spent her nights thinking of how it would be with Tia and that was enough to warm her body right now.

"I'll see you tomorrow. Give your mom a kiss," Gina instructed Carina's kids. Carina's sister smiled and winked, leaving with a trail of kids behind her.

Once everyone was gone Carina searched the front of the house and went to the backyard, finding Tia wiping down the tables.

"You don't have to do that."

Tia shrugged, not swayed by the task, and continued. "I'm not going to leave it here for only you to clean."

Carina sensed that Tia wouldn't stop and decided to join her. Tia began to sing under her breath. Casually, Carina slid to the other end of the table, wiping the chairs and trying to listen. Tia moved around the table, folding one of the chairs and leaning it against the table.

To be stealthy, Carina tiptoed closer to Tia, trying to make out the words. Tia couldn't sing to save her life, but she had a great rhythm flowing. She was headed into the rap part of the song "No Diggity" nodding her head as she let the words flow out.

When Tia turned to move to another table, she leapt back, squealing like she'd been in a horror movie.

Carina couldn't help herself, hunching over in laughter. She covered her mouth and then ran around a table as Tia lunged to grab her. Carina laughed harder, holding her index finger out trying to speak. "I'm sorry." Carina gasped, waving her hands out in surrender. Her eyes teared up.

"No, you're not!" Tia said, crossing her arms over her breasts. She took a step to the side of the table, Carina mimicking Tia's movement. The thrill to grab Carina made Tia take another quick step.

"Wait." Carina snorted, thinking of how bad she'd startled Tia. There was no warning to how loud and high-pitched Tia screamed. "I am. You just sounded so terribly cute."

Tia straightened and narrowed her eyes. She placed her hand over her hips.

Startled by Tia's sudden action, Carina froze unsure what to do. Tia hopped and tumbled off the table into Carina, falling on top of her.

Tackled into the grass, Carina lay underneath Tia, the laughter causing a cramp in her stomach. Tia shifted her weight on top, her knee pressed in between Carina's legs. A moan escaped Carina's lips and the laughter slowly drifted away as they both lie there, mesmerized in each other's eyes.

Carina felt so brave near Tia. She took a chance, hoping Tia wouldn't pull away, and brushed her thumb over her cheekbone. Her heart pounded in her chest. Every part of Carina's body was awake. "Being here with you now...

It's scary, but I know I'm ready to let go of Bruce. I want to move forward with you."

Her eyes dropped to Tia's lips. Carina's breath grew heavy as need spilled out of her. She shifted her head and stole a kiss. It was brief but tender. The feel of Tia's lips made Carina's heart flutter and she tried again. This time, more patient and slower. Her fingers curled into Tia's dreads as she pulled Tia's mouth to hers and kissed her harder. A moan escaped her lips. Carina's stomach tightened as her body felt out of control. The need to breathe was forgotten, and Carina wanted more than a kiss.

Tia pulled back, her hot breath coating Carina's lips, and she shut her eyes. When Tia opened them again, her brown eyes darkened with desire. She'd been holding back and was ready to let go. Tia's mouth crashed into Carina's, pressing her body against hers with a need to be closer.

Carina nipped on Tia's bottom lip, sucking it into her mouth. Carina's hands moved all over, searching for skin to touch. She pulled up the hem of Tia's shirt, slipping her hand underneath, grazing her fingertips over her warm skin.

She felt Tia shudder and continued to work her fingers up her back. Her body yearned for Tia, wanting to explore more of her all night. The butterflies in her stomach seemed to magnify and burst through her body, hitting Carina in her most sensitive spot.

There was nothing more important than this moment. They kissed and explored each other for what felt like hours.

Breathless, they pulled their mouths apart, panting for air.

Carina felt a revelation hit her so hard that tears began to blur her vision. In little over a year of being without Bruce, the friendship and exploration of her bond with Tia had turned into something more. Without realizing it, something had blossomed as they planted a seed into a strong foundation. Carina could see it now.

"You okay? Is this too much? We can—" Tia caressed Carina's cheek with her knuckles.

Carina kissed her again, longingly and hard. She looked into Tia's eyes, pulling away. Tia slid off her, sitting quiet as she waited for Carina to say what was on her mind. There was so much Tia wanted to say, but she wasn't good with her words and she was scared to say it. Tia looked up, gazing into the dark sky. The stars were bright, the moon half full. She shook her arm, pointing up to the sky. "Look, it's a shooting star."

Carina looked up, only catching a second of what Tia witnessed. She smiled and kept her eyes up for a while, star gazing with Tia. This was serene. Carina dropped her gaze to Tia and knew this was only the beginning to something as beautiful and endless as the stars.

Chapter Fourteen

Carina

"So…" Gina waved both hands emphasizing she wanted detail. "Last night. You and Tia were here all alone."

Carina shook her head, hiding her face in her couch pillow. She felt young all over again, thinking of how warm Tia felt. They'd kissed a lot. And talked just as much. This was new and Carina didn't want to over think it. They knew they'd face scrutiny from people who knew Bruce. His family and hers. Friends who would see her and Tia's relationship as inappropriate. Carina loved Tia and facing all those harsh judgments would be worth it.

Gina shook her, trying to get a response. "Come on! I'm trying to get some details and you're stalling."

There was no use in hiding from Gina. She'd keep nagging until she got an answer. Carina lifted her head from the pillow, blowing the few strands of hair off her face. "There's nothing to report. We just talked."

Gina crossed her arms over her chest, narrowing her eyes with suspicion. "Seriously?"

Carina snorted, giving into her sister's inquisitive eyes. "We might've made out several times."

"See…" Gina held her up hand until Carina clapped their hands together. "It's like riding a bike. Well," Gina tilted her head, considering a change in her statement. "In your case, a tricycle."

"Really?" Carina rolled her eyes at her sister's underlined meaning and leaned into the couch, her elbow over the top. She brushed her fingers over her lips, visualizing last night. Tia didn't head home until almost three in the morning.

She'd be at work tonight. Carina was eager to see her but knew she needed to take a chill pill. They needed time apart as much as time they needed time together. In the past, the whole missing each other thing was one of the things Carina loved about dating. To go a few days without seeing the person she wanted to see was both exhilarating and torturous all at once.

"So, when's your first date?" Gina asked.

Carina frowned. "Oh, we haven't gone that far."

"What are you two waiting on?" Gina asked.

Nothing. It slipped Carina's mind. She was only living in the moment not thinking of what steps to take next. Now all Carina could think about was the future. Carina wondered if she should tell her sister she was in love with Tia. There was no need to hide her feelings. "I want to be with her!" After Carina said those words aloud, she looked directly in her sister's eyes searching for support.

Gina smiled, reaching for her hand. "I'd be surprised if you didn't." Her voice held sincerity.

Carina sighed. "You don't think it's too soon?" All Carina desired was to openly own her feelings for Tia.

"What do you think? Because that's all that matters."

"I believe…what we want has no calendar. It's real for her and me. We'll figure out the rest."

Gina nodded. "Then you're on the right track."

*

Tia had been texting Carina throughout the night, sending her flirty messages that made Carina's skin heat every time she read them. The kids were off to bed and Carina was left alone in her room. Carina would be lying if she said she wasn't nervous about their future. Carina wanted Tia. To be intimate with her in the deepest way. Carina just didn't want to disappoint Tia in anyway.

Carina knew sex between them would be magical. She kept telling herself to trust in her heart. It'd been a while since Carina touched herself. A few months after losing Bruce, she needed to think of him until she eventually stopped. Now, all Carina could think about was Tia and she was afraid. Would it be inappropriate to touch herself now? Carina knew she was being ridiculous.

The door was locked, and Carina was naked underneath the sheets. Her heart raced fast with the anticipation of her actions. It didn't hurt to at least try. Carina shut her eyes, imagining Tia coming into her room. Tia sitting at the edge of her bed and running her fingertips down Carina's cheek. Tia's lips on her neck and whispering in her ear before lightly nipping. Carina's hands slid over her belly. She opened her eyes, wanting to picture Tia sliding on top, but her thoughts were short lived. In the corner of her vision, she saw a picture of Bruce and her on the wall.

Carina's hands slid away and her eyes teared up. "Damn it," she groaned and curled to her side. She cried for some time. There was so much more she needed to do in order to move on. If she wanted to make things work for her and Tia, it was time to create change. This was still Bruce's room too.

After several minutes of endless thinking, Carina got out of bed and put on a robe. She walked over to the picture, staring at it and thinking of when this picture was taken. It was one of Carina's favorite days with him. "I have to let you go," she whispered.

Carina's hands shook but she reached up, removing his picture from the wall. Once she took it down, Carina had to take the others down too as well as his poster that he bought at a game store. And the guitar he used to play even though he sucked at. Carina carried them all downstairs into the garage. She did keep one of their pictures in her dresser. She felt there was nothing wrong with keeping one to herself. There were still some pictures of Bruce throughout the house with her and their kids that she'd never put away.

When Carina went back upstairs, she glanced around searching for anything else of his. Carina stared at the bed and realized what stood in her way of potentially being intimate with Tia the most. It was the bed. Carina couldn't keep it and she couldn't sleep on it anymore. Every time she did, it gave her false hope in seeing Bruce again. They'd made memories on this bed. Bringing someone else into it felt wrong.

Carina put on some clothes and walked into Rina's room. She was asleep, an arm dangling over the side of the bed. Carina walked around, stepping over her shoes and slid in beside her. She watched Rina sleep for some time until her eyes shut for the rest of the night.

*

It'd been two days since Carina saw Tia and she was beginning to worry. Tia had been brief in her texts. Carina ended up calling Tia's dad and asking for her address.

Carina didn't consider if Tia would find her action invasive and took a risk. Tia's father told her Tia was sick and right away she got up, grabbed a few things, and headed to Tia's place.

Carina stood in front of Tia's new place, knocking on the door lightly. A woman answered, smiling as she waited for Carina to introduce herself. She was friendly and directed her toward Tia's room.

"Tia," Carina called out, knocking on Tia's bedroom door. Carina smiled to the woman. "Thank you," she whispered.

Carina heard movement inside and stepped back when Tia opened the door, sneezing at the same time. Tia turned her head away, covering her mouth. Her room was stuffy and dark. She'd been sleeping, her eyes fatigued.

"I brought soup," Carina chimed.

"I don't want you to catch what I have," Tia said groggily. "How'd you find my place?"

"Your dad."

Tia nodded. "Sorry I haven't called." Her voice was shredded as if she'd been coughing out a lung.

Carina narrowed her eyes. "You should've told me you were sick. I could've come and taken care of you."

Tia grinned lazily. "Is that what you do for someone you care about?" she asked.

"Yes," Carina said and blushed from Tia's playful question. "Are you going to let me in?"

Tia turned, looking at her room and smiled, embarrassed. "I'm usually not this messy."

"You're sick. And all I care about is you."

She pivoted back, making room for Carina to step in. Tia waved out her hand. "Welcome to my sick domain," she joked.

Tia lazily got back into bed, sliding underneath the covers. "I guess I should let some light in here."

"And air," Carina added. She grinned, twisting open the blinds. The sun wasn't out but the sky still carried enough light into Tia's room.

Tia groaned.

Carina turned, worried something had happened. "You okay?"

"The sun." Tia covered her face with her arm. "It burns." She began to chuckle.

Carina lifted the latch and opened the window halfway. "You're not funny."

"I think so," Tia smiled. Her coughing came sudden and long as she tried to catch her breath. She sat forward until her coughing subsided.

There was cold medicine on the nightstand that was already half empty. Carina placed the soup next to it. A box of tissue was on the floor and she picked it up, offering it to Tia as she took some.

"Sorry. I feel like crap." Tia laid her back against her pillow.

"Have some soup." Carina offered, twisting off the container top. Tia cooperated, letting Carina spoon feed her.

The silence filled the room. When she was full, Tia leaned back, staring at Carina with a furtive grin.

Carina felt Tia staring and looked up. "What?"

"You didn't have to do this."

Two days without Tia had been long enough for Carina. She reached over, brushing her hand up Tia's arm. "I'll always be here."

"I know."

Carina kicked off her shoes and slid into bed. Carina had no intention of leaving Tia alone, and before arriving at

Tia's, she made sure she arranged one of her sisters to watch the kids for the day.

"I don't want you to get sick."

"And I don't want to leave you." Carina sat up, guiding Tia to slide down and lay against her. Carina held her, twirling Tia's dreads around her fingers in an effort to sooth her to sleep. Soon, Tia's breathing drew calm as she relaxed into Carina's arms.

Chapter Fifteen

Tia

"Just admit it." Joe chuckled, chewing on his fourth toothpick of the night. Anytime they had a variety of stressful calls in a row, he'd chew them raw until Tia ordered him to spit them out.

They were parked at the station for the last hour after coming back for a reload of supplies. Their last call was a cardiac arrest that took a handful of their medical supplies. Their parking lot was small with a narrow street on both sides of them. Cars passed by occasionally. It was after 10 at night, the dim street light doing a poor job of keeping them hidden from the overly curious people walking by attempting to take a peek in their ambulance.

Tia pretended not to hear Joe's comment, picking up her phone from the center console. It was too soon to think that far ahead.

"So, you're going to act like I'm not making any sense?" Joe asked in a friendly tone. Tia knew he cared and only had the best of intensions. Her love life wasn't entertainment to him. After getting past her own issues with having a new partner, it was easy to like Joe. He was exactly the kind of partner she needed, and she was thankful he took a chance on her despite the reputation she'd built after Bruce was gone.

"Of course not! I just…" Tia sighed, already feeling defeated, then ran her thumb over her bottom lip and shook her head as if surrendering. Tia hadn't intended to share her thoughts, tonight but Joe was great at pulling words out of her. "It's only been a year since Bruce left."

Joe gave Tia a knowing sympathetic smile but said nothing in regard to her choice of words. She did that a lot, speaking as if Bruce had moved away. She still couldn't say the words aloud for herself to hear.

"I'm sure she's not looking to start dating right away," Tia finished.

Joe grunted. "For a woman, you sure can be blind to what that *woman* of yours wants!" he stated in a tone that made Tia twist her entire body in his direction. For starters, she'd never considered Carina to be hers.

"Medic 111…" a voice over dispatch spoke through the intercom ending their conversation.

Tia straightened, putting her seatbelt on and answering the call. When dispatch alerted them with call status, chills ran up Tia's spine. Her fingers gripped the steering wheel tighter and her breath hitched.

"Medic 113 just got on shift and could easily cover us. Just give the word," Joe whispered in a comforting tone.

Tia hadn't realized she froze, not driving the ambulance yet. She smiled weakly and shook her head. The last thing she wanted was to appear weak. "No. I'm okay."

The call was a hostage situation where a man was holding another person against their will with a gun. Tia mind's instantly thought of Bruce. Instantly, she wanted to fall into a deep hole, but she knew she couldn't.

"All right. I got your back," Joe assured her.

Tia drove to the address in silence, parking a few blocks away. They'd stay parked at a distance until law enforcement detained the suspect.

Over and over again, that night began to play in her mind. The call she received from Carina telling her Bruce had been shot. For the next several minutes, Tia's heart drummed loudly in her ear, anticipating the call that would alert them to come and take the potential gunshot victim to the hospital.

Her brows pinched together fearing the worse. Her fingers gripped the steering wheel tighter as her jaw locked in place. All Tia could think about is how she wasn't there to save Bruce that night. She never missed a shift but the one time she did he died. She'd been working overtime every week and that night she decided to listen to—who? Tia frowned. No, she couldn't blame Carina or Bruce for convincing her to take a night off. She chose to take a night off. It was her own fault. All she had to do was show up and she would've seen that something was off. Tia was good at reading a scene and getting out of a dangerous situation. Bruce would've listened to her, would've left that house and never died that night. Why was she letting this get into her head now?

Warm hands pressed against her shoulders and Tia leapt from her seat, twisting her body sharply. Her arm rose, ready to swing for a punch. She groaned once she realized it was Joe. She blew out a long breath. Of course it was Joe. Tia leaned her head back against the headrest.

"Sorry," she murmured.

Joe didn't say anything right away. Instead he picked up the intercom mic and took a breath. "Copy that. Medic 111, clear from call. Headed back to station."

Tia frowned. She hadn't heard dispatch come on the radio. Embarrassed, she lowered her head. "I didn't—"

"Don't apologize," Joe cut her off. Tia bravely looked his way as he continued. "Don't ever apologize for that." His eyes held hers seriously. "I know what you've been through. You don't have to talk to me about what just happened, but I do think you should tell Carina. She'd want to know."

"I'm sure the last thing she needs—"

"You keep this from her and you'll only isolate her from you all over again," Joe said. He gave Tia a knowing look as if he'd gone through this exact experience. "And, like I was attempting to say earlier, if she wasn't ready to be with you, she wouldn't have made the move. This is scary for both of you. Share that with her and let her in."

Tia sat forward, staring out and considering his words. Perhaps he was right. She sighed and straightened, ready to head back to the station.

*

Carina

The last thing Carina expected to find was Tia pacing on her porch. It was almost seven in the morning, the sun barely exposed through the dark rainy clouds. When the kids told her Tia was outside and hadn't come in yet, Carina knew something was wrong.

After zipping up her jacket, Carina opened the front door and stepped outside. She wrapped her arms around herself, giving Tia the chance to speak first. Something was on her mind and the last thing Carina wanted was to force Tia into speaking. Tia stopped pacing the moment Carina walked out.

A few heartbeats passed when Tia finally looked Carina's way. Her eyes were heavy and guarded. Tia blew out a shaky breath and cleared her throat trying to conceal her emotions. "Do you blame me at all for Bruce…dying?" She struggled to ask, her words breathless. She seemed on the verge of tears.

Mouth agape, Carina frowned unsure of where this was coming from. The last thing Tia needed was random questions thrown her way. She deserved her honesty. Eyes softening, Carina spoke sincerely. "No! I don't."

"Just be honest. I can take it. Even if it was just for a minute I can—"

Carina reached out and grabbed Tia's hands. "Hey," she called out tenderly. She wasn't going to let Tia continue to torture herself with assumptions.

Rain began to trickle down, the front porch overhead protecting them from getting wet. Carina pressed into the door, pulling Tia closer. They were a foot apart when Carina decided to speak. "Where's this coming from?"

Tia sighed. "Work."

"How about we go inside and talk about it?" Carina asked.

Tia suddenly looked nervous. "Are you sure? You didn't plan for my interruption and the kids—"

"The kids are fine. And yes, I'm sure." Carina's expression left no room for misunderstanding.

Tia smiled weakly. "Okay."

Carina didn't let go of Tia's hand as they walked inside the house. Walking through the dining area, they found the kids arguing in the kitchen. Carina halted briefly. "Rina, fix your brother and sister some breakfast. Tia and I are going upstairs to talk."

"Ah mom—" Rina began to whine.

"And please don't interrupt us," Carina added, giving her daughter a serious glare. Carina smiled at Tia and continued down the hall, their hands still laced.

They walked toward the stairs getting ready to head up when Tia hesitated. "Where are we going?" Tia asked in a panicked voice.

"To my room," Carina answered without thought. Carina tried to walk up but Tia didn't move. She turned and peeked from the opening around the hall toward the kitchen where her kids lingered and back to Tia, taking a closer look at the anxiety clear in her eyes. "Hey. Trust me. We're only going up to talk."

Tia felt as if her heart could burst from her chest. "I do trust you. Okay," Tia surrendered.

"Good," Carina said in a playful tone. "Now don't make me drag you up."

Smiling for the first time since arriving, Tia nodded and followed closely behind.

When Carina opened the bedroom door Tia looked into the room before stepping inside. She'd only been in Carina and Bruce's room once. No. This was only Carina's room now. It looked different and felt renewed.

Carina walked inside and spun around to face Tia with an innocent smile. She knew Tia could see the change and wanted to explain. In the past few months Carina had gradually taken Bruce's things out until she finally cleared out practically everything last week. "I have absolutely no idea what I'm doing." Despite Carina's words she was smiling. Being open with Tia felt good. "I was still young when I met Bruce and I know the dating world has changed a lot. But I told you—I'm ready. And you deserve all of me." Carina waved her arms out. "I cleared out Bruce's things. I kept a few things, but overall it's only my stuff and a room for new things to come. I even bought a new bed." Carina noticed Tia's eyes widen. She took a step back, arching a brow.

Leaning on courage, Tia took her first step into the room and sighed. The walls were empty of Bruce's things except for one of his favorite posters. Tia stared up at the Trail Blazers poster Bruce got autographed by the whole team and snorted.

"He showed that poster to everyone for days," Tia grinned, thinking back to that memory.

Carina chuckled. "Every time I look at that poster I smile. He was such a big kid the day he met the Trail Blazers."

Tia continued to glance around until her eyes locked onto Carina's and smiled. There was so much to say but only one thing seemed important. "I blame myself for losing him."

Carina wanted to tell Tia to stop blaming herself and find a way to move on but she knew that would be wrong to say. What Tia felt was real and true for her. Tia didn't need Carina to tell her what to feel. Instead of speaking, Carina grabbed Tia's hand again and guided her to sit on the bed. They sat side by side in silence, Carina comforting her the best she could.

Taking a breath, Tia spoke quietly. "I never missed a shift. And the one time he truly needed me I wasn't there. I was selfish in trying to take time for myself. You have to understand, he wasn't just my partner and brother. We spoke the same language. Bruce and I went on calls just as similar as the one he went on that night. We had each other's back."

The next 15 minutes Tia talked and poured out her emotions and the struggles she endured at work last night.

146

Getting a possible domestic call had ripped open her wounds. When she was done Carina took a moment to take in all her words.

Tia's eyes were heavy with tears ready to spill when she finally looked up. Carina knew this was hard for Tia and didn't want to make it any more difficult.

"This is a lot. I know. The last thing you need is to worry about my feelings." Tia huffed and shook her head. "You have your kids to worry about."

Carina smiled weakly. "Can I share my thoughts?" she asked. Carina had listened and knew Tia needed to hear her response too.

Tia nodded. "Of course."

Sighing, Carina squeezed Tia's hand tightly. "I want you to know—need you to hear me."

Tia nodded.

Carina stared up at Bruce's Blazer poster again and smiled. "I know his death wasn't your fault. He loved you and brought you into our world. And I know, if time could reverse, he wouldn't have wanted you to be there." Carina squeezed Tia's hand tighter. "And I'll always want to hear how you feel. Always."

There was no holding back. Tears fell from Tia's eyes, unsure how to respond. So much pain and grief stood in the way of her happiness and ability to move on completely.

Carina continued on. "Maybe you would've noticed something. Or maybe you wouldn't have and it would've been you who was shot and killed. Or god forbid both of you. Because we both know neither of you would've just watched one get hurt and not react."

Tia groaned, wiping her tears as quickly as they fell. "I would've seen something. Known—"

"Maybe!" Carina said sternly. "But you aren't God or a superwoman who can detect everything around you as much as you try to be."

Closing her eyes, Tia blew out a much needed breath. "I just hate knowing if I'd have been there, I could've seen something."

"All I know is that Bruce wouldn't have wanted you there and even though we never got to say goodbye, he didn't blame you."

This time they both teared up. Tia breathed in heavily feeling a sense of relief roll off her shoulders. They'd never gotten a chance to say goodbye and that was one of the hardest things to handle.

"And for the record, because I see it in your eyes, you aren't stealing me or the kids," Carina spoke softly but firmly. Her words forced Tia to glance up. Carina did her best to hold back tears. She'd always miss Bruce and the life they shared but she needed to move forward too. "Bruce is gone. He died. I had to start saying that out loud to believe it. I know in your head you try to pretend he's somewhere lost at a vacation resort or whatever you tell yourself. But he's gone. And I want to be in love again. And I want that with you. I don't care how that might look in other people eyes. I want to be with you." Carina felt vulnerable but knew she needed to be honest.

"Wow." Tia was speechless. She never thought she'd experience this day. Having someone even mention those words to her seemed only dreamlike. After the life she'd lived, Tia could never settle for anything other than the real thing but thought desiring that was too big a request.

A little over a year ago Carina was happily married to Tia's best friend. Bruce was gone and there was no changing that.

"I want so much for you and the kids," Tia whispered.

Carina slid closer, twisting her body to face Tia and cupped her cheek. There was so much fear in Tia's eyes but Carina knew she'd have to be patient. "And I want so much for us," she stated, hoping Tia could see her truth. Their eyes held for such a long time until Carina's eyes dipped to Tia's lips and the air in the room thickened. There was no denying how much Carina loved her already but she knew Tia wasn't ready to hear that just yet.

"How are you so open and ready after all you've been through?" Tia asked, needing to understand.

Carina smiled sheepishly and shrugged. "Perhaps it's because I've never feared falling in love. Or that I've always been someone who could face my emotions head on without trying to take a detour." On those words Carina gave Tia a sly grin and lowered her hand, linking their fingers together. "It was very hard letting go of Bruce. Even harder telling myself it was okay to love again. His best friend no less."

Tia nodded, expecting many friends and families to voice their oppositions as soon as their relationship was out in the open.

"But most of all," Carina said firmly, squeezing Tia's hand. "You made me want to move forward. You allowed me the space to heal and even cry on your shoulder a number of times. Listen to me bitch and groan about life and its unfairness. Remind me I still have a life to live for. Not just for my kids but for myself."

This time Tia slid her fingers along Carina's cheek and through her hair. Carina leaned into Tia's comforting hand and silently moaned. Her eyes closed briefly, taking in the moment.

"You already had my kids' hearts. I hope that you can one day look at me and want to take mine," Carina said softly, unsure of Tia's reaction. Her eyes were still closed.

Both Tia's hands spooned her face, forcing Carina to gaze up. Their eyes locked for only a brief moment before Tia leaned in ever so slowly.

Carina's heart throbbed in her chest and she moaned before Tia's lips even touched hers. Their mouths inches apart, Tia hesitated as if kissing Carina would release all her control. A few heartbeats passed as their foreheads brushed together. Carina wanted so badly to pull Tia in but knew this had to be Tia's move.

The torture caused Carina to moan louder as their lips almost brushed together. Her lungs felt as if they were suddenly compressed. Heat rippled down to Carina's core. Carina would never forget this moment. This was love and she didn't want to let it pass.

Just as she was expecting Tia to pull away, Tia's lips pressed softly against hers. They both moaned at the same time, breathing heavily. When Tia's mouth opened, Carina teased Tia with her tongue, brushing it lightly over her bottom lip. That seemed to light something deeper inside Tia as she crushed her lips over Carina's.

Carina's hands reached blindly for Tia, needing to feel her skin. When her hands slid in between Tia's thigh, Tia's body jerked in response. Heat emanated from between Tia's legs and Carina gingerly shifted her hand closer to Tia's center.

"Fuck," Tia moaned in dire need.

Carina twisted further into Tia until she ended up on top, pressing her entire body over Tia's longer frame.

Tia lied on her back, legs dangling over the edge of the bed. Her hands found their home, squeezing Carina's inner thighs.

Carina sucked Tia's bottom lip into her mouth, twirling her finger tightly around one of Tia's dreads. "I can kiss you like this forever," Carina panted.

"Please do," Tia said, brushing her lips down Carina's jaw line.

This time Carina didn't wait as she pressed her lips back against Tia's fuller ones. Just as she was about to trail kisses down Tia's neck, Rina burst into the room.

"Mom," she called out in a high-pitched tone. When Rina realized what she walked into, her expression skewed. "Ew, Mom, gross. Your butt's in the air and everything."

Carina squeezed her eyes shut and mentally groaned. Motherhood in all its glories. "Didn't I say not to interrupt us?" Carina said, climbing off Tia who suddenly looked embarrassed. Carina sat next to Tia and looked at her intruding daughter.

"It'd been a while and I figured you guys were just talking about boring adult things," Rina responded. "Plus, Johnathan won't listen to me and eat what I made him," she complained.

"All right, Rina. Just go downstairs," Carina stated. Rina pouted and moved to leave when Carina spoke up. "And later we'll have a conversation about bursting into rooms and following directions."

"But what if Johnathan or Michelle started choking or something? Am I supposed to hope you come downstairs?" Rina asked with attitude laced in her tone.

"And sarcasm. Add that to the list of things to discuss with you, especially since you already know the answer," Carina chastised. "Downstairs. We'll be there in a few minutes."

Rina frowned but said nothing else and walked out, already giving her typical teen attitude. When the door closed Carina grinned weakly at Tia.

"You sure you want to sign up for this?" Carina asked being silly. But soon her eyes held seriousness. "I don't want to ever make you feel like you have to take on this new role in their lives. You're barely adjusting to the idea of us."

"I love those kids," Tia said. She never wanted that to be questioned as well as her intentions toward how much closer they could all become. Tia's heart felt like it was about to implode. There was a lot that she needed to work through. Tia began cracking her knuckles, lifting her head high enough for Carina to see how open she was trying to be. "I hope I'm enough," she ended up saying.

Carina linked their fingers, preventing Tia from cracking her knuckles and smiled. "You are more than enough." Carina could see Tia growing overwhelmed and gently gave Tia's hand a squeeze. "Let's get back downstairs before the kids start tearing my house apart," Carina joked. Without another word they both stood and headed downstairs. In the back of Carina's mind she wondered if Tia would ever let go of her fears and accept the relationship they were establishing.

Chapter Sixteen

Tia

The next two days Tia couldn't seem to catch a breath about her thoughts. The moment Tia left Carina's house after being found pacing like a lost and scared woman, Tia at least hoped she'd work up enough courage to ask Carina out on a date. Joe had been right. Carina knew what she wanted. It was only she who was hesitant.

She found her father sitting on a stool at a bar he frequented. He had a partially empty beer resting next to him. Tia was thankful her father never practiced heavy drinking. Often one addiction could easily lead to a new one. Giving up his life as a gambler was the one thing that ultimately saved their relationship. Tia loved her father despite his flaws. She knew with time and a lot of love he'd eventually come around and he did. Life was where it needed to be between them.

Nodding to the bartender, Tia politely asked for some water and took a seat next to her father. He looked over and gave her a knowing grin.

The only time Tia went chasing her father around in a bar was when she needed to talk. There was a lot on her mind that she finally needed to let out. Tia told herself in several different ways why she was scared to let Carina in completely. Her feelings for Carina were real and yet she couldn't accept it. Because Bruce was her best friend. A brother. Blaming herself for Bruce's death was another major reason. Not being the right kind of person for Carina or the kids. They were all real reasons to her but not the main one.

"You sure you don't want anything stronger?" her father asked. His eyes held concern. "Looks like there's a lot going on in that brain of yours."

Tia smiled weakly. "Can we talk? Privately."

By Tia's tone and plea for privacy, her father could see this was serious. He nodded and stood, placing $10 on the counter.

Thankfully, the bar wasn't packed. That was about all Tia could focus on, narrowing her eyes on the empty small booth in the back corner. She skirted around the other tables as if trying to move around emotional obstacles until she was seated. She finally breathed.

Hands reached out and gripped her balled fists that rested on the table. Tia's father sat on the other end, scooting to the edge of his seat and leaning across the table. "What's wrong?"

The more Tia thought about it, the more it hurt to say the words. When she gazed up at her father she felt a need to cry. She'd put on a brave face for so many years, afraid that if she showed her real feelings it would've delayed his recovery or made him worse. The gambling wasn't the worst part. It was his promises to do better. And better only meant stealing. But her father was strong now. "You know I blamed you for Mom leaving us…so many times," she blew out. "I told myself that if you'd stop gambling and giving us false promises for once, she wouldn't have left." Tia lowered her head for only a second to gather her thoughts and then locked eyes with him again. "Then I hated her for leaving me with you."

All while saying the words, Tia watched her father sit and listen with attentiveness and understanding. His hands continued to grip Tia's firmly. In his eyes, it seemed like he'd been waiting for this a long time.

Saying the words out loud made Tia see all her doubts and fears vividly for the first time. A tear slipped from her eye. "It always feels like I lose the people who matter to me. Whether it's them leaving me, dying, or to addiction. I got you back but I'm always waiting for the inevitable to happen," Tia said honestly. Tia wiped her face as more tears fell.

There was silence for a long moment until her father spoke. "And what all fits into your inevitable doom?" he asked in a solemn tone.

Tia blew out a harsh breath. "Losing Carina and those kids."

He nodded. "Thank you for finally opening up to me. I know how hard that was. I don't take it lightly." Tia had listened to her father countless times ask for forgiveness. And countless times Tia would only brush it off as if his mistakes hadn't hurt her. Tia needed the time to face her feelings.

"I do forgive you!" she finally said.

Her father stifled a sob, covering his mouth briefly with his hand. He then pressed his fingers up to the corners of his eyes, wiping away any oncoming tears. "As much as I want to squeeze you till you beg me to let you go, I know there's more to why you came here." Tia's father knew her inside and out.

"That obvious?" Tia asked.

Her father nodded. "Do you love her?"

Tia's eyes widened and then softened thinking of Carina and the many things she loved about her. She smiled. "So much it frightens me."

"You can either live your life dissatisfied and always questioning your reality or you can live it full of love and spontaneous adventures," her father spoke as if reciting a quote. He smiled. "Tia, don't do what I did. Hoping for things without putting in the work. You love her and I'm betting she feels the same way. Don't give up out of fear of rejection, loss, or something that could possibly happen. Put in the work to get what you've always wanted. A family."

"Dad," Tia said softly. The last thing she wanted was for him to think she didn't consider him family.

He waved her off. "I know, but I think you understand what I'm saying."

Tia sighed. "How do I get past it all?" she asked.

"Step one. Acknowledge what you have with her and own it."

"Own it!" Tia said, sounding brave and hopeful for the first time in almost two days. Tia smiled at her father, knowing what she needed to do. "I think I can do that."

*

Carina

"Will you leave already? You act as if I've never watched your kids," Sandra said, practically shoving Carina out of her own house.

Carina stared dumbfounded by her sister's sudden arrival and "need to relieve her sister of her motherly duties" as Sandra put it. It was almost 11, the sun making a small appearance when Carina ended up standing outside her own home. Sandra gave her a short wave and shut the door in her face. "Really? It's Sunday. I just want to cozy up in my blanket and watch rom-coms."

She heard someone laugh from behind and knew exactly who it was.

Standing several feet away, Tia smiled. "I didn't tell your sister to be that dramatic in getting you out of the house." Tia stood timid for a few heartbeats until she let out a breath. "You said you liked spontaneous moments. I'm hoping I haven't overstepped."

Carina was more confused than ever. "No, but I'd like to be clued in," she said with a grin. She'd missed Tia the last few days. Conversations over the phone didn't seem like enough anymore.

"Well…um…" Tia cleared her throat, eyes steady on Carina as if her response to whatever Tia was about to say mattered. "I thought this was the best time to ask you, if you'd…you know…with me?"

Carina could see her struggle and snorted out of habit from how cute Tia looked right now. It was evident something was on her mind. "Are you asking me—?"

"Will you go on a date with me?" Tia rushed out as if they were playing a game. Tia shook her head. "That's not fair. You made me not say it right."

"You already didn't say it right," Carina teased, closing the distance between them. Before Tia could echo her disapproval, Carina kissed her softly on the lips, running her hands down both sides of Tia's arms. "Yes! I thought you'd never ask."

Tia sighed in relief. "Does now work for you?" She asked with a bit more confidence.

Thankful she dressed up today, Carina shifted a glance toward her house and then back to Tia with a wide smile. "Appears that it does. Perfect timing," she chuckled.

"Good," Tia responded. Tia glanced down at her watch. "Then we should get going before we end up in the far back."

And with that, they were off.

*

Carina

It'd been years since Carina went on a first date. Her nerves had kicked in until she noticed how nervous Tia was. It made her smile. They sat on top of thick blankets Tia provided with one covering both of their lower bodies. A basket filled with food Tia brought was placed in front of them along with a container of chai tea.

Carina wondered what else Tia noticed. The weather was a bit chilly. Thankfully, Tia thought of everything and gave Carina one of her thick sweaters. The sky was grey, the air creating a slight fog. Having a picnic in early March wasn't a normal thing Carina did, but with Tia she'd do this whenever if it meant spending time with her. Other couples and families spread around the open grass field as they looked forward and watched the violinist Lindsey Stirling play. Tia bought the tickets a month ago once she caught onto Carina's love for instrumental music.

All Carina could do was steal a peek at Tia every few minutes. She wanted to be closer. Casually, Carina slid a bit closer to Tia, their arms now brushing against each other.

Tia shifted a glance Carina's way and studied her for a long time until she did the unexpected. Only captured by Carina's presence, Tia's fingers brushed her cheek, grabbing a few strands of Carina's hair and slipping them back underneath her beanie.

Unsure of what action to take, Carina froze, caught in Tia's lingering gaze. Carina's body suddenly became too hot to manage, needing to fan herself from all the built-in desires. There was confidence in Tia's expression that hadn't been there before. And that confidence made Carina want to strip down naked and make love.

"You're exactly what I need," Tia said.

Her words sent a jolt of pleasure between Carina's thighs. When Tia leaned in, Carina thought she'd hesitate, but she didn't. Tia's lips closed around Carina's passionately. Before it could go any further, Tia pulled back and smiled, offering her hand as if she was inviting Carina to run off and explore the world with her.

Carina took it, resting it between Tia's legs. Engrossed by Tia's comfort, Carina rested her head against Tia's shoulder as they watched the musician play.

*

Tia

Their date was a success and they spent most of the day together. It was a quarter to six when they made it to Tia's station. She'd start work soon. They both stepped out of the car, Tia wishing she could call out and spend more time with Carina, but it was too late to ask for anyone to cover her shift.

Carina popped her trunk and Tia went to the back of the car to retrieve her bag. She noticed her ambulance parked out front. The lights were on.

"Should you be helping him set up?" Carina asked.

Tia grinned. "I told him I'd be a bit behind."

"Did you tell him why?" Carina asked in a raspy tone, skirting around her car.

Shutting the trunk, Tia chuckled. "Actually, I did."

Carina's eyes perked up. "Oh, I was joking."

"Was I supposed to keep that to myself?" Tia asked. The last thing she wanted was to screw everything up by running her mouth. She didn't plan on sharing it with the rest of her coworkers but she trusted Joe.

Carina waved off Tia's concern. "It just surprised me that you did at all. Only a few days ago you were hesitant about everything."

"Scared, not hesitant," Tia said, being honest. She sighed. "And I was. I still am. I just don't want my fear to win. I want you more than I want to be afraid." Tia closed the rest of their distance and reached out for her hand. "It feels good being able to tell someone else other than my dad that I'm…" She almost said the words. Chills ran up her spine. "That we're—"

"Together," Carina finished for her.

Tia smiled and nodded. "Together." They were beyond casual dating. It was clear to both of them what they were aiming for.

"I don't care if you scream it to the entire world. As long as you're ready for what might happen," Carina said. She wasn't ignorant to what some people might say but was willing to face those hardships with Tia any day of the week.

Tia nodded. "Whatever happens, I won't deny my feelings for you."

"You better not," Carina teased. She leaned in and kissed Tia's cheek. "You better hurry up before your partner hunts you down. Oh, and perhaps it's overdue on meeting him officially. Invite him to dinner." With that, Carina waved and headed to her car.

Tia watched her drive off and turned to head toward her ambulance. She was nearly there when she heard someone blurt out, "shame," as if he were reenacting the shame scene from *Game of Thrones.*

Twisting around, Tia found one of her co-workers she never got along with standing beside their supervisor. Her brow rose. He'd been one of the countless paramedic's assigned to her unit after Bruce died.

Choosing to ignore him, she walked toward her ambulance and placed her bag inside the middle console.

"Took your sweet time," Joe joked.

Tia rolled her eyes. "I was only saying goodnight to Carina." Once her stuff was placed the way she wanted, Tia slapped the front driver seat. "I need to clock in. Be right back."

Heading for the back station door, Tia punched in the codes and walked inside to find furtive eyes staring at her. They were brief but long enough to know exactly what this was about. Tia waited behind someone else to clock in when the same individual who shouted shame walked in from the other end. He shook his head and rolled his eyes.

"What a shame," he grunted.

This time Tia couldn't hold back. "Is there a problem?" she asked. The back door opened but she didn't see who it was.

"Not unless you're waiting for me to die so that you can go and steal my wife," he muttered.

Someone had seen Carina and Tia, placing the pieces together. Many had already thought it was strange for Tia to be spending so much time with Carina and Bruce's kids, but to end up with her was another big thing that crossed in a few of their eyes.

"Then I guess you shouldn't die," Tia said mockingly.

Joe cut in. "You ready partner?" he asked. "Let's hope I don't croak either. My wife would need all the love and support."

That got a few of Tia's co-workers laughing. As medic's they carried dark humor. But this was more than about being funny. It was about pointing out the obvious and finding the truth.

"Anyone who knows me and knows the connection Bruce and I had shouldn't question my intentions. I don't need to explain myself to anyone. Nor does Carina. Our feelings are real and that's all that matters." Tia nodded to a few people she was work buddies with and walked out of the station.

"You told them!" Joe said.

Tia rolled her eyes and shoved him. "Shut it. Let's make ourselves available."

Chapter Seventeen

Carina

The next three days had been more than Carina could ask for. Tia was home, sleeping after her shift that ended this morning and Carina decided to take the day off. There was a lot on her mind. She hadn't seen her parents since Michelle's birthday party.

On the drive to her parents, Carina promised not to start off by yelling at them. If they didn't want to see her, fine. But to not try and see their grandchildren was a whole other level.

Standing at their front door, Carina no longer felt welcomed and chose to knock.

Several long seconds passed when the door finally opened. Her mother stood with a blanket wrapped around her. She often did that during the cold season. Carina's instinct to lean in for a hug was short lived by the reminder of why she was here. "Carina, honey." Her mother's eyes swayed, unsure of what to say. Her arrival was unexpected. "Your father and I didn't know you were coming." For a brief moment, her mom looked at her with longing eyes until Carina's father approached the door.

His soft face suddenly hardened when he noticed Carina at the door. He wasn't a harsh father, but his faith and conservativeness were the force-fields of his life. "Do you plan to stand in the cold?" he asked. It was his way of inviting her in.

Carina shook her head, seeing that nothing had changed. "I'll keep this short." She stood up straighter. "I don't care what you think of me. Not anymore. But I do care about how you treat my children. They ask to see you and the few times they call, it seems you can no longer stay on the phone long enough to see how they're really doing."

"Hija!" Carina's mother called out.

Carina's hand shot up dismissing her mother's attempt at an excuse. She loved her parents and always would, but her children came first. "You may not understand my relationship with Tia."

"It is a relationship now?" her father asked in a disgruntled tone.

"Yes!" Carina said, leaving no confusion.

Her father huffed. "She was your husband's friend. Do you not see how tainted that is? She probably always wanted you and—"

"Stop it!" Carina hissed in a sharp tone. She didn't care if anyone in the neighborhood walked by and heard them. Carina shook her head, anger boiling out of her. "Don't you dare finish that unwarranted and foul remark. I'm not here for your approval of my relationship with Tia. I've accepted how our relationship has developed. I won't feel guilty for it."

"Your padre doesn't mean to be harsh," Carina's mother said. Her mother was accustomed to always having her husband's back. Carina accepted that a long time ago.

Carina looked at her mother knowing nothing would ever change. Her relationship with her parents had always been great because she'd been living the way they envisioned all her life. Carina didn't realize that until now. When Bruce died, it was like all the pieces that held her relationship with her parents together crumbled apart. It wasn't just Carina being with Bruce's best friend. It was also Tia being a woman. They took it as a grave family insult.

"I'll give you a day to decide if you want a relationship with your grandchildren. Be thankful I'm even giving you this time to really dig deep and consider. My only request is that you keep your opinions to yourself." Carina looked at both of her parents and frowned. "A day," she said and walked off.

*

Tia had come over later in the evening. They all were seated around the couch playing Scrabble. Before Carina had time to realize, a tear slid down her cheek.

Instantly, Tia noticed and gave her a look of concern.

The last thing Carina wanted was to ruin this moment. She wiped her tear and smiled, reassuring Tia she could manage. Another 30 minutes passed when Tia roared in astonishment at Michelle winning the game.

"I guess you'll be doing my English homework from now on," Tia teased.

Michelle giggled. "You aren't in school silly!"

Tia arched a brow. "In three months I will be," Tia chimed out.

Carina gave a questioning look as Tia explained the decision she made. After all this time she finally took Bruce's advice.

Tia put the game away as Carina ordered the kids to go upstairs for bed. They each embraced her and Tia, saying their goodnights, and walked upstairs.

"So, paramedic school," Carina said.

"Yeah," Tia nodded. Tia took a seat on the couch and Carina sat close beside her. "There were a lot of things holding me back before, but none of those things matter."

Carina stared off, getting lost in a memory. "I remember when Bruce went to paramedic school." Realizing she brought up Bruce, Carina sighed. "Sorry, force of habit."

"What are you sorry about?" Tia asked.

"I don't want you to ever feel like I'm bringing him up too much," Carina spoke honestly.

Tia frowned. "Where's this coming from? Don't think I forgot about what I saw earlier." Seeing Carina tear up during their game of Scrabble had been difficult to watch. But she could see that Carina wanted to wait until it was the kids' bedtime to talk.

The last thing Carina wanted was to put too much pressure on Tia, but she knew not telling her would only cause Tia to worry more. "I went to see my parents today."

There was a long moment of silence.

Carina decided to lay her head over Tia's lap and curl into a ball. With one arm tucked under her, she rested her other over Tia's knee. When Tia began to play with her hair, Carina surrendered to the comfort and more tears fell. "I was strong. I gave them an ultimatum, and I hope they listened. I just couldn't allow them to continue to ghost my kids anymore."

Tia sat and listened, continuing to run her fingers through Carina's hair.

She went over everything that was said between them and then blew out a heavy breath. Through all of her anger, Carina was hurt. They'd raised Carina and her sisters. Promised to always be there for her too. "They're my parents," Carina cried.

"Hey, come here," Tia whispered, pulling Carina up into her arms. Tia kissed her forehead and allowed Carina the freedom and support to cry in her arms.

Carina held onto Tia as if she was her life jacket. "I knew they wouldn't understand. It's not like we didn't question it ourselves. Bruce is gone and I'm ready to move on. I feel like that's what we're both doing, right?"

"Yes!" Tia agreed. "We are."

Their eyes locked. "I know we'll face a lot. Not just the opinions of those who feel we shouldn't be together because of Bruce, but also because we're women and kids are involved. God, please watch over the children, right!" This time there was a smile on Carina's face. "I could see it in my parents' eyes. *My kids are doomed because of our lesbian relationship.*" Carina snorted.

"Will they U-Haul next?" Tia added in their playful bantering.

They both began to laugh.

When they were done, Tia smiled. "We already get looks and that will never change. I'm sure me being black and you being Spanish sends further flares up people's noses." Tia's hand brushed Carina's cheek. "But you know what?"

"What?" Carina asked, suddenly mesmerized by Tia's intense eyes.

"I don't care. Because I have you and the kids at the end of the day." Tia's tone was breathless as if every word was an emotional string that played in her heart.

Carina couldn't do this anymore. Hold back the words she needed to say. With the way Tia looked at her, the chances of her not feeling the same way were slim. Carina's heart drummed through her chest. Tears fell from her eyes again. She licked her dry lips and said, "I'm in love with you."

Tia didn't back away. There was no fear or confusion in her eyes. Instead, they darkened with so much raw openness. A smile formed. "I'm in love with you too."

They sat there, amazed and beyond elated. They'd both said the words that mattered most at this moment. There didn't need to be some fancy dinner or romantic scene to say the words. They just needed each other.

When Tia's lips dropped to Carina's mouth, it was all Carina needed to know what would happen next.

Carina's lips crushed over Tia's, moaning with excitement and raw need. Carina's fingers clawed at Tia's clothes wanting to remove them. Her eyes were shut. Blindly, Carina found the hem of Tia's shirt and forced it up over her head until it was removed. Tia wore a sports bra, another obstacle Carina couldn't wait to remove. Tia used her foot to shove the living room coffee table out of their way to make an open space on the floor.

Their lips parted briefly as Carina unbuttoned her blouse slowly. She wanted Tia to enjoy every moment of this. Tia's eyes followed like a predator as each button opened her blouse to reveal Carina's breasts. Tia panted, wanting to touch Carina.

Carina slid the shirt off her arms just as Tia reached in, brushing her lips over Carina's neck. Carina moaned and extended her neck to give Tia more access. Chills flooded Carina's body as heat coursed down her core.

Within minutes both of their clothes were removed and tossed around like unnecessary items. Tia ended up on top, slipping her tongue inside Carina's mouth. Carina replied with a nip at the tip of Tia's tongue. They both moaned from the sensation and warmth of their bodies pressed together. Tia's fingers grazed Carina's clit and she jolted from the pleasure. Tia sucked Carina's nipple into her mouth, causing her to moan louder.

When Tia's fingers brushed over Carina's clit again, this time she lifted her hips to feel the pressure of Tia's teasing fingers.

"Wait. No," Carina blew out breathless. "I want to touch you first," she panted. "No cheating."

Tia snickered. "This," Tia said, moving her finger in a circular motion all the way around Carina's opening. Carina shuddered an erratic breath. "Isn't cheating," Tia said.

"Tia, I swear I will hurt you if you tease me like that again. Not on this round," she said trying to regain some control. Her eyes were shut. "I want to come with you. I need that," she whispered.

Tia understood. She'd never felt this before and the last thing Tia wanted was to neglect in any way the love making they were experiencing. "I'm with you," Tia whispered, meaning her words.

They stared into each other's eyes, both vulnerable and brave. Tia positioned herself over Carina to give her access to her most intimate self as she could feel Carina a few inches from her fingers.

It was as if they were one. Both of their fingers slid inside the other as a wave of pleasure was gladly welcomed from both of them. Carina fought the need to cry out as Tia instantly slid a second finger in. Her body tried to rock into every stroke of Tia's fingers but was forced to stay in place from Tia's body pressed over her own. Tia moaned and leaned down as they kissed long and passionately. Tia gasped when Carina stroked her opening faster. Tia gripped Carina's hair as her fingers moved inside of Carina faster.

Their bodies shuddered uncontrollably at the same time as they experienced a combined orgasm.

Tia's body relaxed into the floor as she processed their love making. Part of her was in shock. Some part of Tia hadn't realized that her relationship with Carina was real until this moment. Touching and kissing her felt dreamlike, but making love and all that came with it was no fantasy. Tia mumbled, "Damn, that was…unexpected."

"Yeah," Carina nodded. "We're creative people." Carina giggled, twisting on top of Tia's naked body. Her chin pressed into Tia's upper stomach, arm draped over her waist. "That was amazing. Hot." She maneuvered completely on top and pressed her lips against Tia's. "You awoke every part of me that I could go for more right now."

"Next round will be all about you," Tia grinned, running the tip of her finger down Carina's back.

Carina shuddered. "Yes, but upstairs behind doors. Luckily we had this couch covering us."

"Right!" Tia smiled. "Upstairs."

They both grabbed their clothes and snuck upstairs to make love until sleep finally took them.

Chapter Eighteen
Four Months Later

Carina

Mid July was always hot with mild humidity. All Carina desired during this time of the month was a cold drink and a foot massage by a pool. Last summer had been so emotional; Carina looked forward to spending genuine time with her kids and Tia this year.

Carina's parents had stepped up four months ago after Carina confronted them and since the kids weren't in school because of summer break, they spent time with them frequently.

Today was Carina's annual family picnic but this year Carina was hesitant to go. She hadn't spoken personally to her parents in months. Rina had told her grandparents that if Tia couldn't come she wouldn't go. Carina's parents backed down, making no fuss over Carina bringing Tia as her girlfriend. They'd been happy and Carina had no intention of ruining a good day by forcing Tia to come if she didn't want to. She just wouldn't show up either. But as they sat in the kitchen for breakfast, Rina looked at her mom, hoping Tia would say yes.

"I said I would talk to her, honey," Carina said to her daughter for the fourth time. Carina sipped lightly on her tea, noticing her daughter's intense stare.

"Mom, I know you," Rina said. "You'll mention it, but then tell Tia you don't want to go when I know you do.

Family is everything to us. You taught us that," Rina argued. "And I know Grandma and Papa are being idiots—"

"Hey," Carina cut in.

"They are and you know it," Rina said. "I love them, but they are. Besides, today isn't about them. We have cousins and aunties and uncles whom you get along with perfectly fine that will be there. Don't let Grandma and Papa take this day away from you."

When did Rina grow up? She'd be 13 soon enough. Carina smiled, proud of her daughter's maturity. Many of her family did support her. After they'd found out about Tia and her, they sent a bunch of lesbian cards in the mail. Silly ones. Their funny way of saying they loved and supported her. "All right. I'll really talk to her. But please know this will be hard for her too."

"I know," Rina nodded.

"Who wants donuts!" Tia shouted coming inside the house. She walked through the kitchen holding out a box. Her grin was big and Carina could tell Tia loved spoiling her kids.

Carina narrowed her eyes. "Sugar?" she said. "They're already about to be filled with sweets," Carina pointed out.

"Yeah, so why not start the day off on sugary fun," Tia explained.

"I concur," Johnathan said grabbing two donuts.

When did he learn that word? Carina thought. Her kids were growing up way too fast.

Tia placed the box on the counter, pulling out a chocolate glazed donut. It was Carina's favorite and Tia knew it. She waved it near Carina's face and grinned. "I suppose you don't want any then," Tia grinned.

Carina narrowed her eyes playfully. "Evil," Carina muttered under her breath.

Casually, Tia brushed her lips over Carina's and then handed her the donut. "How are my four favorite people?" Tia asked offering her arms to take turns giving each of them a hug.

"Good," was all Michelle could utter, mouth half full of her donut. Her eyes looked bigger than her stomach, staring at the donut as if it was a quest she had to complete.

"Can I hang out with you instead?" Johnathan asked Tia randomly.

Tia frowned and snuck a peek at Carina for an explanation.

"No!" Rina rushed out. She looked to Carina ready to pout if she didn't ask soon.

Carina hadn't mentioned her family's picnic to Tia, convinced she wouldn't want to attend. The last thing Carina wanted to do was make Tia feel like she had to face her parents glare only to be judged and possibly mistreated for being in love with their daughter. Besides, Carina had no intention of going until Rina made it very clear she wasn't going to attend without them. Carina knew Rina looked forward to this every year and didn't want to take that away from her.

"It's my family's annual picnic," Carina finally stated. Her smile was tight and forced, seeing her kids' nervous eyes wander between the two of them.

"The one you invited me to last year?" Tia asked.

Carina nodded.

Tia stood quiet for a long moment. "Then don't let me stop you guys from missing all the fun. I knew the kids were headed to their grandparents. Just didn't know it would be that kind of a wild adventure." Tia was being strong for the kids. She looked to them with big eyes. "You three don't look ready to leave," Tia pointed out.

Tia was getting better at giving silent suggestions that alerted Carina she wanted to talk privately.

"That's very true," Carina agreed. "You three should be getting ready. I know your grandparents will want you and all your cousins over for a sleepover so pack an overnight bag."

Michelle slid out of her seat with her donut sitting on the napkin she used as a plate. She looked stuffed and sighed. "I can't finish it," she said as if disappointed with herself.

"That's all right. I'll finish it for you," Tia assured.

Rina gave her mom one last plea reminder with her eyes and then headed toward the stairs.

Johnathan seemed to be the only one left hesitating to get up. His behavior had improved in the last several months, but today he was struggling to speak, keeping his head down. "I'd rather stay home."

"Johnathan, the video games can wait," Carina stated. Every chance Johnathan got, he asked to play. Since summer break started, Carina had been pushing him to go outside more and socialize. "Right now I need you to go upstairs and get dressed."

"Fine," he blew out harshly and stormed up the stairs.

Carina shook her head. She'd let him calm down for now and discuss things later.

Finally alone, Tia took the seat closest to Carina and positioned to face her, making it evident that she wanted to talk.

"I know what you're going to say," Carina said. "I should've told you."

"Why didn't you?" Tia asked, reaching in to grab hold of Carina's hand.

Carina sighed. "Because my parents haven't treated you with any respect, and I didn't plan on going."

"I'd never tell you to disown your parents for me," Tia said. She appreciated how much Carina cared, but she didn't want her to one day regret not speaking to her parents again because of their relationship.

"First, they've done a great job at making me feel disowned all on their own." There was bitterness in Carina's tone but she was working through it. One day at a time. "Second, you're someone I'm very proud to be with. And I'll never regret not going where we both aren't welcomed." Carina's attempt at maintaining composure was quickly failing.

Tia smiled and nodded. "Do you want to go?" Tia asked.

Carina gave it some thought. She took in a long breath and leaned into her seat. "I've always loved going. There are so many who still support me and my life. But it won't be the same," Carina said honestly. "I have all the family I need in this house," Carina said, staring into Tia's eyes. "The rest can just see me when my parents aren't around."

Tia nodded. "But?" she said, knowing Carina well.

"But Rina really wants both of us there. I explained to her why she shouldn't expect you to jump for joy at the idea. Maybe she's just being a teen, ready to face her grandparents for social justice or something," Carina joked.

Tia chuckled. "Maybe," she said rolling her eyes. "I can see her now holding up a protest sign, demanding equality."

They both laughed.

Carina silenced first, staring down at their linked fingers. "I'll tell her it's all too much and—"

Tia shook her head, preventing Carina from continuing. "No!" she said adamantly. Their eyes locked. "I chose all of you. That meant those kids up there too. I fell in love with you because not only are you an amazing woman—passionate and honest—but also because you're an amazing mother." Tia squeezed their linked fingers. "For whatever reason, Rina needs us there. So, I say yes and to hell with your narrow-minded parents."

Carina snorted. "Understatement." She looked into Tia's eyes for the longest moment. A tear slid from Carina's eye and marked a passage down her cheek. "I love you."

*

Tia

The entire car ride to Carina's family picnic felt emotionally draining, but Tia held it together for the kids and Carina. Despite Carina putting on a brave face too, Tia wasn't oblivious to her fears. Tia was fortunate to never be treated differently or unwanted by her father when she came out to him years ago. More than half of Tia's gay friends had parents who no longer talked to them for choosing to be their true selves. Tia admired Carina's strength. To have been happily married to a man and create three children with him only to openly explore her feelings for a woman after such a devastating loss took a lot of guts.

Carina's hand squeezed Tia's thigh, drawing her attention toward their present surrounding. The car was parked in front of a volleyball court someone must have set up for the event.

Tia noticed the huge picnic shelter with a banner stretched across it. It read *30th Castillo Annual Family Picnic.* Tia's brows rose. "You weren't joking when you said this was tradition."

"Yeah. Normally, they don't put up some big banner. Only every 10th anniversary," Carina explained.

Tia twisted to see the kids were already out of the car. She hadn't realized she'd zoned out long enough for them to exit.

"We can leave whenever," Carina promised.

"Same goes for you too," Tia said. She opened her passenger door and smiled before exiting the car. If they lingered any longer Tia was afraid they'd never get out.

Carina walked around the car, meeting Tia on the sidewalk, and offered her hand.

Tia arched a brow and nodded toward many of Carina's family already taking notice of them. "You are a badass!" Tia said with pride.

Carina snorted. "I'm only walking up to my family with the woman I love just like any other couple here would do and has done."

Tia took hold of Carina's hand and smiled. Her heartbeat could almost be heard with every step they took. Relief slowly settled into Tia's bloodstream when she noticed most of Carina's family eager to greet them. Tia recognized a few from last year and from Michelle's birthday party. Their kind and supportive eyes made Carina let out an audible sigh as she hugged her relatives.

Carina introduced Tia to everyone that surrounded them and conversation began to flow immediately. When Carina's sisters approached, it was evident to Tia that despite what Carina thought, she'd needed to be here too. Tia understood how much Carina loved being a part of a big family. For Tia, it had always been only her and her father.

There was well over 40 people here with just over a dozen kids of various ages running around. Carina had warned her that today would include a lot more people than last year and Tia suspected more would arrive.

"Would you like something to drink?" Carina's sister Sandra asked. She opened the ice chest near where they'd sat.

"A Sprite would be great actually," Tia answered.

Tia knew that in the beginning there had been hesitation in Sandra's support. She was relieved that whatever objections she had before were dissolved. Casually, Tia noticed from the other end of the picnic shelter Carina's parents sitting with their backs turned to them. A few other members of Carina's family sat with them, probably gossiping about Tia's presence.

"I hope you know I'm happy my baby sister was able to open her heart up again," Gina said. She'd been observing Tia for several long heartbeats.

Tia gave Gina's words some serious thought. "I don't plan on going anywhere." This time Tia snuck a peek at Carina who was also glancing her way. They locked eyes and smiled. Carina had fallen into a deep conversation with her other sister and cousins.

"No one expects you to," Gina said, pulling Tia's attention back to her.

Tia gave her a furtive glance and chuckled lightly. "I doubt that."

'Well," Gina said, apologetically. "They don't count."

"Yes they do," Tia admitted. She wasn't trying to challenge Gina's words. She knew Gina was only trying to make her feel comfortable. "But I can live with that as long as Carina can."

"You're right and I'm thankful Carina has you by her side," Gina said.

"What are you two talking about?" Carina asked playfully, moving around the bench to sit next to Tia.

Carina followed Tia's brief line of sight and sighed. "I didn't come here for them. I came here to see the people who have my back no matter who I am. And my kids deserve to still have their family."

"Amen to that," one of Carina cousins cheered, holding up her soda. Everyone followed along and cheered, continuing their conversations with lighter topics for the next hour.

Tia could see why Carina loved her family so much. She'd never been apart of something like this herself and only hoped she'd be able to share more moments like this for all the years to come.

When Carina finally stood to guide Tia to meet more of her family that had arrived, they were instead greeted by Rina rushing to their side with a look of bad news to report.

Chapter Nineteen

Carina

"What's wrong?" Carina asked immediately. She knew her daughter's expressions well enough to know it involved one of her siblings.

Just as Rina was about to speak, one of the boys about Johnathan's age walked up with tears in his eyes and a bloodied nose.

All the adults took in the boy's appearance as his father called out to his son, using his shirt to stop his nose from bleeding. The father, Piero, was one of Carina's distant cousin's she only saw during events like this. Carina frowned, already sensing where this was headed. More of the kids walked up with stories eager to tell.

Tia noticed Michelle and called her over. Michelle moved swiftly to Tia's side, hiding her body from the other kids by standing behind Tia.

The boy started sobbing, telling his dad what had happened.

Carina ignored the boy and looked around for Johnathan. "What happened?"

"Where is your son?" Piero called out to Carina as if she answered to him.

"Back off," Sandra ordered.

Carina continued to glance around in search of Johnathan. The more time went by the more concerned Carina became. "Rina, where is your brother?"

Tears flooded Rina's eyes. "I don't know!" She rushed out.

This time Tia spoke up. "I'll go check the playground," she said, running in that direction.

"He hit me," the boy staggered through a frustrated breath.

"You deserved it," Rina argued, defending her brother.

Almost three months without an outburst. Carina thought Johnathan was doing better. He'd been smiling more than ever and generally at peace with all he'd endured. He must've been provoked.

"No kid should be hitting anyone. Especially my son," Piero argued.

Carina noticed her parents approaching, sensing the trouble.

"Why do you think he deserved it?" Carina asked Rina.

Michelle began to cry now. Carina moved toward Michelle and knelt beside her, soothing her daughter. "What's wrong, honey?" Carina asked softly.

She looked at the boy who'd been punched in the face by Johnathan. "He was saying mean words to me and Johnathan told him to leave me alone but he didn't."

"That's a lie," the boy hollered.

Carina could see Tia coming back without Johnathan and gradually, panic began to suffocate her.

"NO, it's not," Michelle argued with defiance. "Just like last week when he and his older brother kept picking on Johnathan calling him a homo." Michelle said the last word with confusion.

"I never—"

The boy tried to argue, but Piero cut in. "Shut it." He looked to Carina with embarrassment. "I'm sorry. My son clearly crossed a line."

Carina was no longer focused on hearing what happened, watching Tia jog back without Johnathan at her side. Worry began to creep even closer, filling her lungs. "Nothing?" Carina asked Tia when she approached.

Tia shook her head.

"Is this why he didn't want to come today?" Carina asked her eldest.

Rina nodded.

Carina groaned, wishing she would've noticed something earlier and asked questions. Right now that didn't matter. She couldn't afford to panic. "We need to find my son," Carina said.

Everyone agreed, Sandra organizing everyone to split up and search the entire park. This was the last thing Carina expected to happen today. She needed Johnathan to be safely found.

"I want to help," Rina blurted out.

"I need you to take care of your sister," Carina stated, trying to sound in control.

Tia reached out, cupping both sides of Carina's face. In the softest voice Tia whispered, "I need you to take a breath. We'll find him."

The park was huge with a river nearby. A thought clicked to mind. "Bruce and Johnathan use to go fishing up the river."

"We can send your father—" Carina's mother offered.

Carina shook her head. "No! I need to be the one searching for him."

"Oh, Carina. Stop all this worrying. You're scaring the girls," Carina's father muttered. "I remember when you and your sisters use to—"

"I won't stop worrying," Carina sneered. Anger spilled out of Carina and she was no longer able to contain it. "He lost his father and now he's out there because I told him he'd be in trouble if he continued his poor behavior. I made my son too afraid to come to me. And I won't chill or stop all my worrying…" Carina said in a sarcastic tone "…until he is in my arms."

"Perhaps you shouldn't have flaunted your new inexcusable lifestyle in your child's face," Carina's father bit back.

"Hey," Tia called out. "I think you should go."

"This is family—"

Carina cut her father off. She wasn't naïve as to why Piero's son called Johnathan that insensitive word. It had everything to do with Carina being with Tia but she'd never apologize for it. "Actually, Tia is my family."

Carina noticed Sandra coming their way without good news. "I think I know where he went. I need you to take my girls and I'll call as soon as we have him."

"Mom," Rina complained.

Michelle began to cry again.

Tia bent down, kissed Michelle's forehead, and reached out for Rina to take her hand. "You know I have everyone's back. I need you two to have each other's and let your mom and I bring Johnathan home."

After a moment, they both nodded.

Carina sighed in relief, hugged her girls, and then watched Sandra guide them away. Without bothering to say anything to her parents, Carina pointed to the car. "It'll be faster by car." Tia nodded and they were off.

*

Tia

It took them 10 minutes to arrive at the other end of the park. The Willamette River was long, but Bruce had only taken Johnathan to one spot near this park. They walked briskly, glancing everywhere. The park was less occupied with people, only a few pulling their kayaks out of the water. Further up were large boulders that resided against the river's edge.

Tia felt so overwhelmed with the need to find Johnathan that her body shook with adrenaline and anxiety.

"I can't find him," Carina said, voice cracking.

"We will," Tia said, reaching over to grab Carina's hand and look along the rocks. Kids liked to climb down too close to the edge. Just as they were about to turn back and head in the opposite direction, Tia shouted, "There he is!"

When Carina's eyes landed on her son sitting along the rocks she sighed. They were 30 feet from him when Carina decided to call out his name. "Johnathan!"

His small frame straightened and he turned to face his mother. Fear sprung in his eyes until he noticed his mother's wide smile.

Tia could see that Johnathan expected his mother to approach with anger and frustration over him running off. Instead he was greeted with love and relief.

Johnathan stood with tears in his own eyes.

They were only a few feet from him. "Come here, sweetie."

Johnathan tried to step around one of the bigger rocks but his legs were too small. Without warning he lost his balance. It was as if the world was suddenly moving in slow motion. Carina screamed as Johnathan's body fell into the river.

"Call 911!" Tia shouted. Tia didn't think; she just reacted. Out of pure instinct, Tia moved across the rocks and dove into the water. Her body was numb to the temperature, only focused on finding Johnathan. She could hear Carina in the background but couldn't make out any words. Jonathan hadn't resurfaced and Tia submerged under the dark and murky water.

Tia's arms stretched out blindly for Johnathan pleading with the universe to help find him. When she came up for air, Tia could see Carina hunched over the water, tears in her eyes. People gathered around offering to help Carina, while some pulled out their phones to record. Thoughts of the night Bruce died flashed briefly in her mind. Tia couldn't afford to give up. Taking in another long inhale, Tia went back under knowing she wouldn't come out of this water until she had Jonathan in her arms.

The water was about 10 feet deep where Tia swam so she decided to move further out to follow the current. Tia stopped counting how long she'd been under, relying on the dire need to find Johnathan to keep her breath held. Tia couldn't see and the water stung her eyes. She decided to close them and rely on faith and instinct to guide her to Johnathan. Her body felt as if her insides were being compressed from a lack of air. Tia mentally fought through the panic and swam lower, stretching her arms, when suddenly her fingers enclosed around what she hoped to be Johnathan's arm. He didn't resist as Tia pulled him close, his body pressed against her. Tia worked hard to swim to the surface, pleading for Johnathan to be alive.

Tia gasped for air the moment her head reached the surface. Warm air touched her wet face. Tia made sure Johnathan's head was above water and began swimming toward Carina's screaming voice.

"Take him," Tia said, coughing harshly. She held him up as someone helped Carina pull Johnathan from out of her arms.

When Tia could finally see clearly, she looked up to find Piero's hand and took it. Tia's body moved with determination to reach Carina who laid out Johnathan beside her. She was checking his airway.

"I don't think he's breathing," a random voice said in a horrified tone.

Tia dropped to her knees, immediately beginning CPR. She knew he wasn't breathing. She'd checked for a pulse right before Johnathan was pulled out of the water and hadn't felt a breath come out of him when she purposely placed the palm of her hand over his mouth.

"Carina, two breaths after I finish a round of 15." Tia guided her, counting her compressions in her head.

Tia stopped and Carina moved into action, providing her son with mouth-to-mouth airway breathing.

"Tilt his head back a bit more," Tia guided Carina properly.

As soon as Carina finished with the second breath, Tia began CPR again. She could hear sirens and knew that paramedics would be on scene in the next minute. Tia twisted to see an ambulance pull into the park. It was Medic Unit 72, a crew she knew well and trusted.

Tia stopped compressions again and allowed Carina to give two breaths. Tia jumped back into action, looking across Johnathan's body to Carina who was sobbing and running her fingers through her son's hair. Tia couldn't let Carina lose Johnathan too. "He's strong. We got this," Tia rasped out to Carina, needing her to keep her faith.

Carina nodded. Tia stopped just as the medic crew walked up, pulling out a bag valve mask and an oxygen tank. They cranked it up high and connected the tubes, placing it over Johnathan's mouth and nose.

"Tia we should take—"

"No," Tia shouted. "I can keep giving compressions. One of you work on airway and set up an I.V.," she ordered.

One of the crew pulled out an AED, and Carina sobbed looking from each medic to Tia who stopped long enough for them to cut off Johnathan's clothes and dry him off. They placed small defibrillator pads over his chest and covered him with a blanket. Tia looked up at Carina unsure if she should let them work on Johnathan without her so she could comfort Carina or continue helping.

Instinct drew Tia back into action right in time to continue compressions. For every press into Johnathan's chest Tia made, she pleaded for him to wake up. She couldn't lose him too. This time she was here and could help.

Anger took hold of her as she stopped and stared down at Johnathan's unmoving body. Tia blinked out tears and when it was her turn again, she began talking to Johnathan. "I love you. Wake up. Your mom and sisters need you. I need you."

The paramedic to her left patted her shoulder. "We're checking for a rhythm."

Tia moved back far enough to keep a safe distance incase Johnathan's heart needed to be shocked. She focused only on Johnathan, not listening to anything.

"He's aspirating," Tia said calmly, tilting his body to the side. Water poured from his mouth and puddled on the ground beside him. Tia and another medic straightened him and checked for a pulse. "He's breathing," Tia said in sudden relief.

"Tia…" one of the medics whispered to her.

She nodded. "Go," she said, slowly standing and moving out of their way.

Carina moved to her side. "I want to go—"

"I'll drive us to the hospital," Tia encouraged. She knew there was a chance for Johnathan to go into cardiac arrest while on the way to the hospital. When it came to intense calls like this, medic crews preferred not to have parents in the ambulance in case they freaked out. Carina watched them place her son on a gurney and hesitated. Tia held Carina's face. "Look at me."

"No," Carina argued. "If I can't go, then you go."

Tia wanted to be with Carina but she knew Carina needed her to be with Johnathan. If Tia could give her any comfort then she would.

"I'll take her," Piero said, motioning to Carina.

Carina watched her son be loaded into the ambulance and Tia could see what she feared most at that moment. Neither of them got the chance to say their goodbyes when Bruce was killed. That couldn't be their fate again.

"I'll see you soon," Tia promised and moved toward the ambulance, alerting them she'd sit up front.

They nodded and she hopped inside, looking through the rear-view mirror as Carina watched them leave.

Chapter Twenty

Carina

Watching Tia leave with Johnathan was one of the hardest things Carina had to do. So many thoughts ran through her mind. She tried not to let fear cloud her and reminded herself to stay strong. Piero had guided her to his car and before Carina could pay attention to her surroundings, they were at the hospital.

Carina climbed out of the car and walked through the double glass doors of the emergency room. It was the same one Bruce had taken his last breath in. She noticed Tia standing in the waiting room pacing around. Carina ran up to Tia, gripping her arm. She needed to know where her son was. "Johnathan?" she asked, afraid of Tia's response.

"He did well in the ambulance. Woke up. They're still working on him though," Tia assured.

She looked exhausted and drained. Carina looked her over and frowned. "You need to get out of these wet clothes," Carina advised.

"I'm fine," Tia said, shrugging off Carina's concern.

Carina pulled Tia away from the doors where a doctor would step through to bring them news. "Please, Tia. Don't have me worry about you too."

Tia looked at Carina, finally acknowledging her words and nodded. Without warning she began coughing heavily. After several long seconds, Tia took a few slow, deep breaths and groaned. "Okay. I'm okay," she said. "I'll get some scrubs from one of the nurses."

Carina watched Tia walk up to the nurse's station, getting let through and guided to where she could change out of her wet clothes.

"Carina!" her mother's voice rushed out, walking quickly toward Carina as she sat down. Her father and sisters followed closely behind.

"Where's Rina and Michelle?" Carina asked.

Sandra reached in for a hug. "With my husband. They're okay. Just worried about their brother."

"What happened?" Carina's father asked, needing to know the details.

Carina didn't have the strength to tell them anything. All she could think about was her son. Occasionally, she looked toward the door, expecting a doctor to come out at any minute. The memories of the last time she was here passed through her mind. Seeing the look on the doctor's face right before telling her that Bruce had died.

Carina hadn't realized she was shaking until her mom wrapped her arms around her in comfort. The argument from earlier seemed to no longer matter. Accepting her mother's support, Carina twisted, finally allowing herself to breathe just a little. Only enough to see her through this.

Her head jerked up when Tia walked back toward her with a small smile on her face. Everyone looked to Tia as if she had answers. In a ragged sigh, Tia's smile widened as her eyes lingered on Carina. "He's okay. They said he's asking for you." As if the world was finally becoming stable again Carina collapsed into Tia's arms, sobbing with relief. Tia held her tightly. "He's okay. They're running a few tests and will be out soon," she whispered in Carina's ear.

The family gathered around them and celebrated.

Carina and Tia finally chose to sit, eager to see Johnathan. Carina rested her head against Tia's shoulder. "Thank you," she whispered for only Tia to hear.

"I wasn't going to quit. I would've kept swimming..." Tia's words fell silent.

Carina lifted her head and stared into Tia's eyes. "I know." Their lips touched as a tear slid from Carina's eye.

"Thank you for saving my grandson." Carina's father spoke. He stood a few feet from them, looking at Tia with polite intent.

Tia nodded. "I love Johnathan and I'll always be there for him and the girls."

"And my daughter, it seems," he stated. His tone wasn't rude but he didn't smile.

Carina was sure it'd take a while longer before her father either learned to accept her relationship with Tia or stayed stuck in his ways.

A doctor came out into the room and everyone stood as he approached. Soon Carina and Tia were headed into Johnathan's room. When they walked inside Johnathan's eyes widened, happy to see them. Carina moved around the bed quickly and hugged her son for the longest time. She'd lost one person in this hospital and was thankful not to lose another.

"Mom, you're squeezing me too hard," Johnathan complained.

"No such thing," Carina said, cheerful. Happy tears fell.

Tia moved to the other end of the bed, giving Johnathan a long and hard kiss on his forehead.

"Gross," he whined through the oxygen mask placed around his face.

"You scared me to death," Carina said. She knelt close to him, looking him in the eye. "I never want you to fear being honest with me. I'll always love you know matter what you do."

Johnathan nodded, eyes watering. "Love you, Mom!"

"Love you too!" she said softly.

They talked to Johnathan for some time until the family started to visit one by one. It was late when everyone stopped coming and clearing out for the evening. Johnathan was asleep in the bed.

Carina looked toward her son every time he stirred and smiled with much relief.

Leaning back into the chair in Johnathan's room, Tia wiped her eyes as if fighting off sleep.

"Maybe you should—"

Tia didn't let Carina finish her words. "I'm not leaving you or the kids. Work and my apartment can wait."

"Actually, I was going to say maybe you should stay home with the girls tonight." Carina smiled weakly. "They're only allowing one person to sleep here tonight and Johnathan can leave in the morning at the earliest. Besides, I know Rina and Michelle are worried and want to be home. They need you."

Tia's brows lifted. "Oh," she said, surprised by the suggestion. "I thought we were keeping sleepovers only for nights we were alone."

"That was your suggestion, remember?" Carina pointed out.

Tia nodded. "I suppose you're right."

Carina reached over and linked their fingers together. "I'm not asking you to move in just yet," Carina grinned. "But I don't see your home being anywhere except with us. We're your family." The way Carina looked at Tia there was no mistaking her words.

For the first time tonight, Tia finally understood what it was like to have a family to go home to. Picturing it now, Tia let warmth settle into her heart. Reaching out, Tia offered her hand. Carina took it as Tia squeezed it tightly. She peered over to Johnathan sleeping and then closed her eyes, thinking of the girls she'd pick up tonight from Sandra's house.

Losing Bruce was the hardest thing Tia had faced. He'd given her the opportunity to know his family and through that, find love in an unexpected way. She'd never forget him and would always honor his memories. Tia was finally ready to let go of lingering fears and accept the new life waiting for her.

Tia's eyes locked onto Carina, confident in what she needed. She'd never give them up. She loved them all. "I have every intention of building a life with you and those kids. My love for you is bigger than anything I've ever experienced and I'll always love you."

They grinned at each other as Carina closed the distance between them, brushing her lips over Tia's. This is what love felt like. Warmth, excitement, and need.

A love as *'Endless as the stars.'*

About the Author

Domina Alexandra is a native of Southern California who has recently transplanted to Salem, Oregon. She is an author of stories with strong female protagonists, authentic emotions and thrilling action scenes that mirror her career as an EMT on the way to becoming a SWAT Medic. She grew up writing poetry as an outlet and, in 2006, joined a Live Theater program, where she played many roles in productions of plays and musicals. During her four years of acting, she fell in love with writing monologues, screenplays, and all things story. When she's not saving lives as an EMT, she advocates for LGBT Youth with a vision of growing a stronger community of care, acceptance, and compassion. Her books include *Her Endure*, *I Belong with Her*, *A Night Claimed*, *Love Undercover,* and *Omega Rising.* She gets her imaginative ideas from her life as a EMT as well as being stuck in her head too long as a child.

Other Titles Available From
Triplicity Publishing

Change of Seasons by J. C. Smith. Professor Lynn Maxwell knew that the accident would change her life. What she couldn't have anticipated is that it would lead her to the kind of love she had always wanted but never imagined. Lori Bowman, having known Lynn for most of her life, became first her caretaker and now so much more. Having survived a painful past, Lori has become the woman she hoped to be. The one who deserves to be with Lynn. Caring for Lynn gives her the chance to return the care she had received for so long. Moving through adversity together has deepened their relationship, and Lynn and Lori anticipate their bright future together. The one thing Lynn is concerned about is how her daughter Beth will respond to the relationship. But could someone else be a bigger threat?

Bittersweet and Sparrow by Kathy L. Salt. Rathmoria Emporie, 1719. Sparrow Stonehill, a street walker, is forced into life on the run when her house of employment is bombed overnight. Between a brutal oppressive leadership and an equally violent revolution - where is her place? What side is she on in the civil war? And what does Astrid Dace, the alluring general of the revolution, want with her? A love story set in a fictional industrial age dystopia; Bittersweet and Sparrow is the exciting first installment in the Waerdarei-series.

Crossed Reins by Graysen Morgen. Barrel racing is Carly Rae Walsh's life, until it's ripped out from under her. With nothing to do and nothing to lose, she uses her years of horse whispering skills and intuition to train a troubled thoroughbred race horse. Allison McKinley is a world class dressage rider who has stepped back from the spotlight to mourn the sudden death of her mother. The last thing she needs when she decides to start training again for competition, is her father's impulsive desire to own a race horse, and his bizarre decision to choose a rodeo barrel racer as the trainer. The two women have nothing in common except horses, and even that's a stretch. Can they uncross the reins long enough to see what's happening between them?

Outside In by Breanna Hughes. Cali Evans is a survivor. Her life hasn't been easy, but her late father raised her to be smart, tough, and dependent only on herself and her wits. On the eve of her 21st birthday she meets Owen Bray - a beautiful and intriguing young doctor who equally frustrates and captivates Cali. That fateful meeting inspires Cali to make a better life for herself. The next day, hoping to make positive change, Cali hops a bus for the West Coast but never reaches her destination. Instead, she wakes up in an underground bunker with no recollection of how she got there. Upon her arrival, she learns that she's one of just forty survivors of a fast-spreading environmental toxin and that human life outside of the bunker has ceased to exist. Tired of the vague explanations and half-answers coming from the people in charge, Cali takes it upon herself to investigate the real reason why she's there and begins to uncover the sinister truth.

I Love You, Nora Whispered by Kathy L. Salt. Love in the time of horses and polio. England, 1948. Nora Lakes suffers from post polio syndrome and very low self-esteem. When her sister Martha manages to get her a job at Waterhouse Acre Stables, she can hardly believe it. She had never imagined that anyone would have employed her, damaged as she is. She also never imagined she would meet anybody like Katherine. Katherine Waterhouse was born with a silver spoon in her mouth. She has a mean streak and doesn't like people in general. What she does like, is horses. She wants to be a professional rider but growing up in a conservative house where her choices are limited by her sex, Katherine has always been trapped in her role as a woman. Nora and Katherine - two women with very different backgrounds, drawn to each other with an intensity neither of them are prepared for. Do they stand a chance?

Omega Rising by Domina Alexandra. A few months of peace. That was all Bonnie Collins was granted. New trouble has surfaced and go figure, this trouble came with a new pair of claws. When an unknown pack comes to town, Bonnie is forced to make tough decisions that will influence her packs future. Things only get harder when her mate is taken, leaving Bonnie in charge of a pack who still doesn't trust her. With chaos all around, it will be exactly what Bonnie needs to finally embrace what she has become. An Omega Rising. Book 2 of the *Claimed Series*.

Loose Ends by Joan L. Anderson. After her estranged sister is killed when she falls onto the subway tracks in Paris just as a train arrives, Allison goes to Paris to deal with her sister's body and collect her things. But, after talking to the police about the accident and viewing the subway surveillance video, something seems odd about her death. When Allison's hotel room in Paris is broken into with only a few things taken, but not any money or credit cards, she begins to wonder if it really was an accident that killed her sister, or if it was murder. Once Allison returns to Washington, D.C. to handle her sister's affairs, she soon realizes that her sister had been living a secret life and wasn't the person she had always thought she was. As troubling things begin to happen to Allison in D.C., she starts wondering if she will be the next person to die.

Real Love by Graysen Morgen. Leigh Myer is a trauma nurse practitioner who is not happy going through the motions of her daily life. When a friend offers up her mountain cabin for a relaxing vacation, Leigh packs her bags. She's never been to the mountains and certainly never in heavy snow. A chance meeting with a fish and wildlife officer turns her idea of a quiet, relaxing vacation…upside down. Camden Gorely loves her job and loves the mountain she works and lives on even more. She's tired of having flings with vacationers who visit for days or weeks at a time, until she meets the elusive nurse from the city. Can Leigh stop running from her past and allow real love into her heart?

Enticed by Love by Lynn Lawler. Henrietta Bailey is a mysterious woman who has spent her entire life living in the town of Crescent, a sleepy beach community in central coastal California. She loves the beach, the ocean air, and the town itself. Her simple life fulfills her. However, she spends much of her time reminiscing about her long-lost love, a woman who left her devastated. Now, another woman awaits on the horizon; a wise, intelligent, and sexy lady who is sophisticated beyond her years. This woman yearns for her soul mate and lover. Will she be able to win

Henrietta's heart, or will Henrietta be fated to live the rest of her days alone?

Love Undercover by Domina Alexandra. Remi Stone never expected to get the opportunity to work undercover for narcotics. But, when the chance arrives, she takes it. With drugs coursing through a high school, Remi has only until the end of the school year to find the suspects responsible. Undercover, Remi plays her role, moving one step further into the drug industry. She never thought she'd be moving one step closer to the woman who would change her life and take hold of her heart. There is just one issue. Remi Stone is undercover as an eighteen year old high school senior. And the woman she can't seem to ignore is her History teacher. There will be a lot of challenges along the way, including one that could cost Remi her life and her heart.

Playing the Game by Graysen Morgen. Randi Rojas is a professional soccer player who seemingly has it all, a successful career, a long-term girlfriend, a loving family, and a great group of friends…until a chance meeting with an attractive woman sends her way offside, and into a whole new game. Berkley Ward lives her life to the extreme, spending her days either in the gym or four-wheeling in the woods, and her nights patrolling the streets as an officer. Affairs with taken women are easy, but after years of playing games, she's finished…until she meets a beautiful woman and a game she can't resist. Both women play a dangerously seductive game of cat and mouse, teetering on the edge of friendship and affair.

Rebel Sweetheart by Sydney Canyon. When a headstrong, country music superstar starts getting threatening letters while on tour, her manager has no other choice but to hire someone to investigate the threats, and keep her safe. Haley Nielsen is as stubborn as it gets. She does things her way, and her way only. The last thing she needs or wants is a babysitter following her every move and controlling everything she does. Shane Crowley isn't your typical private investigator, or bodyguard, for that matter. She's a former U.S. Deputy Marshal with a lot of experience, and an all or nothing attitude. Tempers flare and the energy burns red hot between the two women as they spend weeks together cooped up on Haley's tour bus, traveling the country. Will they stop resisting each other long enough to see eye to eye? Or will the letter writer make good on his threats?

A Tale of Spiders and Canned Soup by Kathy L. Salt. Living on your own can be hard, but even more so when you're dealing with haphephobia; the death of a twin sister; and a crush on your teacher. Mika is still in contact with her foster family who homes the loves of her life, three young children she would do anything for, when she begins attending University of Aberdeen and meets Pauline, an Australian that teaches Viking history. Neither woman is used to breaking the rules, and their way to each other is a hard one, especially when Mika vows to get custody of the children, whether she is ready to be a parent or not. *A story about growing up. A story about dealing with grief. A story about Mika and Pauline.*

A Night Claimed by Domina Alexandra. Bonnie Collins had plans. And being a werewolf wasn't one of them.

Attacked by a rogue who was out to claim her, and facing what she now has no choice of becoming, Bonnie can't let go of her human life as a Paramedic. The last thing Bonnie needs is more challenges. However, Rikki, the Alpha of Mill City will be just that. Finding her to be possessive and ruling, Bonnie begins challenging the Alpha's every breath. Finding out her attack was no accident only makes her more angry at the situation. A group of rogues are out to get her. With no clue why, Bonnie has no choice but to seek help from the alluring Alpha and her pack, accepting the new world she was forced into.

Stunted by Breanna Hughes. Professional stuntwoman Jessie Knight takes her job very seriously and although she works in the entertainment industry, she has zero desire for fame or notoriety. She also has a very strict no-dating policy when it comes to coworkers. That is, until, she meets famous actress Elliot Chase on the set of her new film. The adrenaline rush of the stunts is nothing compared to the sparks that fly between them. After a passionate night together, a sex tape is leaked that sends Jessie and Elliot's private and professional lives into a spiral. Will the fallout be too much for them to last? Or will they find a way out of the mess together?

Mission Compromised by Graysen Morgen. Natalia Moreno is thrilled when she arrives in Fiji for a relaxing vacation. However, she soon discovers the overwater bungalow she's staying in has been double booked for the entire stay, and the resort is full. Annoyed and frustrated, she has no other choice but to share her hut with a stranger. Christian Garnier is sent to Fiji for what she refers to as a working vacation, until she finds out she has an ornery roommate for the next two weeks who is dead set on making her job twice as hard. Soon, all hell breaks loose and the two women are sent around the world on a wild goose chase.

Stargazing by Kathy L. Salt. Lissa stared open-mouthed at the GIF that played over and over on the screen in front of her. Heat flushed to her face, igniting her skin. Her heart started pounding in her chest. *Stupid internet, it should really come with a warning label.* She's never been interested in relationships or sex and as the years have gone by she has retreated more and more into her work. Everything changes when she meets Star, a porn actress with a heart of gold and a troubled childhood. *They say that opposites attract, but how much of that is true? What chance do they have when one of them is a virgin and the other one star in pornography?*

I Belong with Her by Domina Alexandra. Tajel Pierce loves the thrill of being a paramedic. Every call she goes on gives her a rush. She makes no time for a personal life. No one can ruin her love for her career. Then there is Arianna Castaldi, who just transferred to her new paramedic position in a whole new state. All she needs is a new start without any distractions. Arianna and Tajel's relationship doesn't start off perfect. Embarrassed of the one night stand Arianna believes she had with Tajel, she wants to pretend they never met and make their relationship strictly business. The only choice they have to keep from strangling each other is to go from denying their feelings to accepting them as they work through intense 911 calls.

Awakened by Fate by Lynn Lawler. Jackie is a woman living life according to her own rules. She's married, but it's the unspoken, open kind. She can have as many female lovers as she likes; she just can't talk about them. After a bizarre encounter turns her world upside down, things slowly begin to change. She finds herself in desperation as she searches for answers. What she discovers is nothing is delivered in a neatly wrapped box. Now that everything has been brought out into the open, she finds she can't run away from her truth anymore. With her new life, comes new responsibilities and a different outcome than what she was expecting. Jackie isn't alone in the story. She meets several new people who help her along her journey.

Nautical Delights by S. L. Gape. Lady Elizabeth Barrington has spent her entire life trying to please her family; constantly opting for a quiet life, she utilises her profession as a doctor to keep out of her families' clutches; bar the annual two-week Caribbean private cruise, where there is simply no budge. Confined to two weeks on board the Iconica super yacht, she intends on keeping her head down and enjoying as much of the holiday as she can, whilst keeping her family at arm's length. Until a crew member catches her eye.

Worlds Apart by S.L. Gape. Hollywood A-lister Heidi Spencer-Brady is everything you'd expect of an Idol. Loved by all, the British Beauty is graceful, talented, humble and so far removed from the 'typical' LA scene. When her husband's infidelity with his new 'leading lady' is leaked, Dawn, Heidi's best friend and manager, goes all out to protect her. She arranges for Heidi to go back to the UK and stay on her cousins farm they had visited as children, much to the disappointment of the animal fearing Heidi.

Castor Valley (Law & Order Series Book 2) by Graysen Morgen. Jessie Henry is torn when she reads about the capture of the Doyle brothers, two young men who were part of her old gang. Unable to let them hang for a crime she's sure they didn't commit, Jessie leaves her wife and the Town of Boone Creek behind, and sets out on a journey back to the one place she thought she'd never see again, *Castor Valley*. Ellie Henry watches the love of her life leave, not knowing if she will ever return. When she gets an odd telegram, nearly a week later, she fears Jessie is in trouble. With no other choice, she goes to the one person who can help her.

Fight to the Top by S. L. Gape. Georgia is a forty year old, single, Area Director from Manchester, UK who is all work and definitely no play. Having no time to socialise or spend time with her family she prides herself on being fit and well-polished. Erika is an Area Director for the same company, but in the United States. Whilst she is concentrating so heavily on the promotion she has been fighting for, she's starting to feel like her life outside of work is falling apart. The two women are exceptionally different, and worlds apart. Both of their lives are turned upside down when their jobs are snatched from under their noses, and they are suddenly faced with being thrown together by their bosses for one last major project...in Texas.

Boone Creek (Law & Order Series book 1) by Graysen Morgen. Jessie Henry is looking for a new life. She's unknown in the town of Boone Creek when she arrives, and wants to keep it that way. When she's offered the job of Town Marshal, she takes it, believing that protecting others and upholding the law is the penance for her past. Ellie Fray is a widowed, shopkeeper. She generally keeps to herself, but the mysterious new Town Marshal both intrigues and infuriates her. She believes the last thing the town needs is someone stirring up trouble with the outlaws who have taken over.

Witness by Joan L. Anderson. Becca and Kate have lived together for eight years, and have always spent their vacation in a tropical paradise, lying on a beach. This year, Becca wanted to try something different: a seven day, 65-mile hike in the beautiful Cascade Mountains of Washington state. Their peaceful vacation turns to horror when they stumble upon a brutal murder taking place in the back country.

Too Soon by S.L. Gape. Brooke is a twenty-nine year old detective from Oxford, who has her life pretty much planned out until her boss and partner of nine years, Maria, tells her their relationship is over. When Brooke finds out the truth, that Maria cheated on her with their best friend Paula, she decides to get her life back on track by getting away for six weeks in Anglesey, North Wales. Chloe, a thirty three year old artist and art director, owns a log cabin on Anglesey where she spends each weekend painting and surfing. After returning from a surf, she stumbles upon the somewhat uptight and enigmatic Brooke.

Never Quit (Never Series book 2) by Graysen Morgen. Two years after stepping away from the action as a Coast

Guard Rescue Swimmer to become an instructor, Finley finds herself in charge of the most difficult class of cadets she's ever faced, while also juggling the taxing demands of having a home life with her partner Nicole, and their fifteen year old daughter. Jordy Ross gave up everything, dropping out of college, and leaving her family behind, to join the Coast Guard and become a rescue swimmer cadet. The extreme training tests her fitness level, pushing her mentally and physically further than she's ever been in her life, but it's the aggressive competition between her and another female cadet that proves to be the most challenging.

Never Let Go (Never Series book 1) by Graysen Morgen. For Coast Guard Rescue Swimmer, Finley Morris, life is good. She loves her job, is well respected by her peers, and has been given an opportunity to take her career to the next level. The only thing missing is the love of her life, who walked out, taking their daughter with her, seven years earlier. When Finley gets a call from her ex, saying their teenage daughter is coming to spend the summer with her, she's floored. While spending more time with her daughter, whom she doesn't get to see often, and learning to be a full-time parent, Finley quickly realizes she has not, and will never, let go of what is important.

Pursuit by Joan L. Anderson. Claire is a workaholic attorney who flies to Paris to lick her wounds after being dumped by her girlfriend of seventeen years. On the plane she chats with the young woman sitting next to her, and when they land the woman is inexplicably detained in Customs. Claire is surprised when she later runs into the woman in the city. They agree to meet for breakfast the next morning, but when the woman doesn't show up Claire goes to her hotel and makes a horrifying discovery. She soon finds herself ensnared in a web of intrigue and international terrorism, becoming the target of a high stakes game of cat and mouse through the streets of Paris.

Wrecked by Sydney Canyon. To most people, the *Duchess* is a myth formed by old pirates tales, but to Reid Cavanaugh, a Caribbean island bum and one of the best divers and treasure hunters in the world, it's a real, seventeenth century pirate ship—the holy grail of underwater treasure hunting. Reid uses the same cunning tactics she always has before setting out to find the lost ship. However, she is forced to bring her business partner's daughter along as collateral this time because he doesn't trust her. Neither woman is thrilled, but being cooped up on a small dive boat for days, forces them to get know each other quickly.

Arson by Austen Thorne. Madison Drake is a detective for the Stetson Beach Police Department. The last thing she wants to do is show a new detective the ropes, especially when a fire investigation becomes arson to cover up a murder. Madison butts heads with Tara, her trainee, deals with sarcasm from Nic, her ex-girlfriend who is a patrol officer, and finds calm in the chaos of police work with Jamie, her best friend who is the county medical examiner. Arson is the first of many in a series of novella episodes surrounding the fictional Stetson Beach Police Department and Detective Madison Drake.

***Mommies (Bridal Series book 3)* by Graysen Morgen.** Britton and her wife Daphne have been married for a year and a half and are happy with their life, until Britton's mother hounds her to find out why her sister Bridget hasn't decided to have children yet. This prompts Daphne to bring up the big subject of having kids of their own with Britton. Britton hadn't really thought much about having kids, but her love for Daphne makes her see life and their future together in a whole new way when they decide to become mommies.

Rapture & Rogue by Sydney Canyon. Taren Rauley is happy and in a good relationship, until the one person she thought she'd never see again comes back into her life. She struggles to keep the past from colliding with the present as old feelings she thought were dead and gone, begin to haunt her. In college, Gianna Revisi was a mastermind, ring-leading, crime boss. Now, she has a great life and spends her time running Rapture and Rogue, the two establishments she built from the ground up. The last person she ever expects to see walk into one of them, is the girl who walked out on her, breaking her heart five years ago.

Second Chance by Sydney Canyon. After an attack on her convoy, Marine Corps Staff Sergeant, Darien Hollister, must learn to live without her sight. When an experimental procedure allows her to see again, Darien is torn, knowing someone had to die in order for this to happen. She embarks on a journey to personally thank the donor's family, but is too stunned to tell them the truth. Mixed emotions stir inside of her as she slowly gets to the know the people that feel like so much more than strangers to her. When the truth finally comes out, Darien walks away, taking the second chance that she's been given to go back to the only life she's ever known, but she's not the only one with a second chance at life.

Meant to Be by Graysen Morgen. Brandt is about to walk down the aisle with her girlfriend, when an unexpected chain of events turns her world upside down, causing her to question the last three years of her life. A chance encounter sparks a mix of rage and excitement that she has never felt before. Summer is living life and following her dreams, all the while, harboring a huge secret that could ruin her career. She believes that some things are better kept in the dark, until she has her third run-in with a woman she had hoped to never see again, and gives into temptation. Brandt and Summer start believing everything happens for a reason as they learn the true meaning of meant to be.

Coming Home by Graysen Morgen. After tragedy derails TJ Abernathy's life, she packs up her three year old son and heads back to Pennsylvania to live with her grandmother on the family farm. TJ picks back up where she left off eight years earlier, tending to the fruit and nut tree orchard, while learning her grandmother's secret trade. Soon, TJ's high school sweetheart and the same girl who broke her heart, comes back into her life, threatening to steal it away once again. As the weeks turn into months and tragedy strikes again, TJ realizes coming home was the best thing she could've ever done.

Special Assignment by Austen Thorne. Secret Service Agent Parker Meeks has her hands full when she gets her new assignment, protecting a Congressman's teenage daughter, who has had threats made on her life and been whisked away to a Christian boarding school under an alias to finish out her senior year. Parker is fine with the assignment, until she finds out she has to go undercover as a Canon Priest. The last thing Parker expects to find is a beautiful, art history teacher, who is intrigued by her in more ways than one.

Miracle at Christmas by Sydney Canyon. A Modern Twist on the Classic Scrooge Story. Dylan is a power-hungry lawyer who pushed away everything good in her life to become the best defense attorney in the, often winning the worst cases and keeping anyone with enough money out of jail. She's visited on Christmas Eve by her deceased law partner, who threatens her with a life in hell like his own, if she doesn't change her path. During the course of the night, she is taken on a journey through her past, present, and future with three very different spirits.

Bella Vita by Sydney Canyon. Brady is the First Officer of the crew on the Bella Vita, a luxury charter yacht in the Caribbean. She enjoys the laidback island lifestyle, and is accustomed to high profile guests, but when a U.S. Senator charters the yacht as a gift to his beautiful twin daughters who have just graduated from college and a few of their friends, she literally has her hands full.

Brides (Bridal Series book 2) by Graysen Morgen. Britton Prescott is dating the love of her life, Daphne Attwood, after a few tumultuous events that happened to unravel at her sister's wedding reception, seven months earlier. She's happy with the way things are, but immense pressure from her family and friends to take the next step, nearly sends her back to the single life. The idea of a long engagement and simple wedding are thrown out the window, as both families take over, rushing Britton and Daphne to the altar in a matter of weeks.

Cypress Lake by Graysen Morgen. The small town of Cypress Lake is rocked when one murder after another happens. Dani Ricketts, the Chief Deputy for the Cypress Lake Sheriff's Office, realizes the murders are linked. She's surprised when the girl that broke her heart in high school has not only returned home, but she's also Dani's only suspect. Kristen Malone has come back to Cypress Lake to put the past behind her so that she can move on with her life. Seeing Dani Ricketts again throws her off-guard, nearly derailing her plans to finally rid herself and her family of Cypress Lake.

Crashing Waves by Graysen Morgen. After a tragic accident, Pro Surfer, Rory Eden, spends her days hiding in the surf and snowboard manufacturing company that she built from the ground up, while living her life as a shell of the person that she once was. Rory's world is turned upside down when a young surfer pursues her, asking for the one thing she can't do. Adler Troy and Dr. Cason Macauley from Graysen Morgen's bestselling novel: *Falling Snow*, make an appearance in this romantic adventure about life, love, and letting go.

Bridesmaid of Honor (Bridal Series book 1) by Graysen Morgen. Britton Prescott's best friend is getting married and she's the maid of honor. As if that isn't enough to deal with, Britton's sister announces she's getting married in the same month and her maid of honor is her best friend Daphne, the same woman who has tormented Britton for years. Britton has to suck it up and play nice, instead of scratching her eyes out, because she and Daphne are in both weddings. Everyone is counting on them to behave like adults.

Falling Snow by Graysen Morgen. Dr. Cason Macauley, a high-speed trauma surgeon from Denver meets Adler Troy, a professional snowboarder and sparks fly. The last thing Cason wants is a relationship and Adler doesn't realize what's right in front of her until it's gone, but will it be too late?

Fate vs. Destiny by Graysen Morgen. Logan Greer devotes her life to investigating plane crashes for the National Transportation Safety Board. Brooke McCabe is an investigator with the Federal Aviation Association who literally flies by the seat of her pants. When Logan gets tangled in head games with both women will she choose fate or destiny?

Just Me by Graysen Morgen. Wild child Ian Wiley has to grow up and take the reins of the hundred year old family business when tragedy strikes. Cassidy Harland is a little surprised that she came within an inch of picking up a gorgeous stranger in a bar and is shocked to find out that stranger is the new head of her company.

Love Loss Revenge by Graysen Morgen. Rian Casey is an FBI Agent working the biggest case of her career and madly in love with her girlfriend. Her world is turned upside when tragedy strikes. Heartbroken, she tries to rebuild her life. When she discovers the truth behind what really happened that awful night she decides justice isn't good enough, and vows revenge on everyone involved.

Natural Instinct by Graysen Morgen. Chandler Scott is a Marine Biologist who keeps her private life private. Corey Joslen is intrigued by Chandler from the moment she meets her. Chandler is forced to finally open her life up to Corey. It backfires in Corey's face and sends her running. Will either woman learn to trust her natural instinct?

Secluded Heart by Graysen Morgen. Chase Leery is an overworked cardiac surgeon with a group of best friends that have an opinion and a reason for everything. When she meets a new artist named Remy Sheridan at her best friend's art gallery she is captivated by the reclusive woman. When Chase finds out why Remy is so sheltered will she put her career on the line to help her or is it too difficult to love someone with a secluded heart?

In Love, at War by Graysen Morgen. Charley Hayes is in the Army Air Force and stationed at Ford Island in Pearl Harbor. She is the commanding officer of her own female-only service squadron and doing the one thing she loves most, repairing airplanes. Life is good for Charley, until the day she finds herself falling in love while fighting for her life as her country is thrown haphazardly into World War II. Can she survive being in love and at war?

Fast Pitch by Graysen Morgen. Graham Cahill is a senior in college and the catcher and captain of the softball team. Despite being an all-star pitcher, Bailey Michaels is young and arrogant. Graham and Bailey are forced to get to know each other off the field in order to learn to work together on the field. Will the extra time pay off or will it drive a nail through the team?

Submerged by Graysen Morgen. Assistant District Attorney Layne Carmichael had no idea that the sexy woman she took home from a local bar for a one night stand would turn out to be someone she would be prosecuting months later. Scooter is a Naval Officer on a submarine who changes women like she changes uniforms. When she is accused of a heinous crime she is shocked to see her latest conquest sitting across from her as the prosecuting attorney.

Vow of Solitude by Austen Thorne. Detective Jordan Denali is in a fight for her life against the ghosts from her past and a Serial Killer taunting her with his every move. She lives a life of solitude and plans to keep it that way. When Callie Marceau, a curious Medical Examiner, decides she wants in on the biggest case of her career, as well as, Jordan's life, Jordan is powerless to stop her.

Igniting Temptation by Sydney Canyon. Mackenzie Trotter is the Head of Pediatrics at the local hospital. Her life takes a rather unexpected turn when she meets a flirtatious, beautiful fire fighter. Both women soon discover it doesn't take much to ignite temptation.

One Night by Sydney Canyon. While on a business trip, Caylen Jarrett spends an amazing night with a beautiful stripper. Months later, she is shocked and confused when that same woman re-enters her life. The fact that this stranger could destroy her career doesn't bother her. C.J. is more terrified of the feelings this woman stirs in her. Could she have fallen in love in one night and not even known it?

Fine by Sydney Canyon. Collin Anderson hides behind a façade, pretending everything is fine. Her workaholic wife and best friend are both oblivious as she goes on an emotional journey, battling a potentially hereditary disease that her mother has been diagnosed with. The only person who knows what is really going on, is Collin's doctor. The same doctor, who is an acquaintance that she's always been attracted to, and who has a partner of her own.

Shadow's Eyes by Sydney Canyon. Tyler McCain is the owner of a large ranch that breeds and sells different types of horses. She isn't exactly thrilled when a Hollywood movie producer shows up wanting to film his latest movie on her property. Reegan Delsol is an up and coming actress who has everything going for her when she lands the lead role in a new film, but there one small problem that could blow the entire picture.

Light Reading: A Collection of Novellas by Sydney Canyon. Four of Sydney Canyon's novellas together in one book, including the bestsellers Shadow's Eyes and One Night.

Visit us at www.tri-pub.com